PALE HORSE,
PALE RIDER

THREE SHORT NOVELS

Books by Katherine Anne Porter

Flowering Judas and Other Stories
Pale Horse, Pale Rider
The Leaning Tower and Other Stories
The Days Before
The Old Order
Ship of Fools
The Collected Stories of Katherine Anne Porter

PALE HORSE, PALE RIDER

THREE SHORT NOVELS

KATHERINE ANNE PORTER

A Harcourt Brace Modern Classic

Harcourt Brace & Company

New York   San Diego   London

For information about permission to reproduce selections from
this book, write to trade.permissions@hmhco.com or to Permissions,
Houghton Mifflin Harcourt Publishing Company,
3 Park Avenue, 19th Floor,
New York, New York 10016.

www.hmhco.com

Library of Congress Cataloging-in-Publication Data
Porter, Katherine Anne, 1890–1980.
Pale horse, pale rider: three short novels/Katherine Anne
Porter.
p.   cm.—(A Harcourt Brace modern classic)
ISBN 0-15-170755-3
Contents: Old mortality—Noon wine—Pale horse, pale rider.
I. Title   II. Series.
[PS3531.O752P3   1990]
813'.52—dc20   89-26886

Designed by Michael Farmer
Printed in the United States of America
DOH 22
4500821143

To Harrison Boone Porter

CONTENTS

OLD MORTALITY

She was a spirited-looking young woman, with dark curly hair cropped and parted on the side, a short oval face with straight eyebrows, and a large curved mouth. A round white collar rose from the neck of her tightly buttoned black basque, and round white cuffs set off lazy hands with dimples in them, lying at ease in the folds of her flounced skirt which gathered around to a bustle. She sat thus, forever in the pose of being photographed, a motionless image in her dark walnut frame with silver oak leaves in the corners, her smiling gray eyes following one about the room. It was a reckless indifferent smile, rather disturbing to her nieces Maria and Miranda. Quite often they wondered why every older person who looked at the picture said, "How lovely"; and why everyone who had known her thought her so beautiful and charming.

There was a kind of faded merriment in the background, with its vase of flowers and draped velvet curtains, the kind of vase and the kind of curtains no one would have any more. The clothes were not even romantic looking, but merely most terribly out of fashion, and the whole affair was associated, in the minds of the little girls, with dead things: the smell of Grandmother's medicated cigarettes and her furniture that smelled of beeswax, and her old-fashioned perfume, Orange Flower. The woman in the picture had been Aunt Amy, but she was only a ghost in a frame, and a sad, pretty story from old times. She had been beautiful, much loved, unhappy, and she had died young.

Maria and Miranda, aged twelve and eight years, knew they were young, though they felt they had lived a long time. They had lived not only their own years; but their memories, it seemed to them, began years before they were born, in the lives of the grown-ups around them, old people above forty, most of them, who had a way of insisting that they too had been young once. It was hard to believe.

Their father was Aunt Amy's brother Harry. She had been his favorite sister. He sometimes glanced at the photograph and said, "It's not very good. Her hair and her smile were her chief beauties, and they aren't shown at all. She was much slimmer than that, too. There were never any fat women in the family, thank God."

When they heard their father say things like that, Maria and Miranda simply wondered, without criticism, what he meant. Their grandmother was thin as a match; the pictures of their mother, long since dead, proved her

4

to have been a candle-wick, almost. Dashing young ladies, who turned out to be, to Miranda's astonishment, merely more of Grandmother's grandchildren, like herself, came visiting from school for the holidays, boasting of their eighteen-inch waists. But how did their father account for great-aunt Eliza, who quite squeezed herself through doors, and who, when seated, was one solid pyramidal monument from floor to neck? What about great-aunt Keziah, in Kentucky? Her husband, great-uncle John Jacob, had refused to allow her to ride his good horses after she had achieved two hundred and twenty pounds. "No," said great-uncle John Jacob, "my sentiments of chivalry are not dead in my bosom; but neither is my common sense, to say nothing of charity to our faithful dumb friends. And the greatest of these is charity." It was suggested to great-uncle John Jacob that charity should forbid him to wound great-aunt Keziah's female vanity by such a comment on her figure. "Female vanity will recover," said great-uncle John Jacob, callously, "but what about my horses' backs? And if she had the proper female vanity in the first place, she would never have got into such shape." Well, great-aunt Keziah was famous for her heft, and wasn't she in the family? But something seemed to happen to their father's memory when he thought of the girls he had known in the family of his youth, and he declared steadfastly they had all been, in every generation without exception, as slim as reeds and graceful as sylphs.

This loyalty of their father's in the face of evidence contrary to his ideal had its springs in family feeling, and a love of legend that he shared with the others. They loved to tell stories, romantic and poetic, or comic with a romantic humor; they did not gild the outward circumstance, it was the feeling that mattered. Their hearts and imaginations were captivated by their past, a past in which worldly considerations had played a very minor role. Their stories were almost always love stories against a bright blank heavenly blue sky.

Photographs, portraits by inept painters who meant earnestly to flatter, and the festival garments folded away in dried herbs and camphor were disappointing when the little girls tried to fit them to the living beings created in their minds by the breathing words of their elders. Grandmother, twice a year compelled in her blood by the change of seasons, would sit nearly all of one day beside old trunks and boxes in the lumber room, unfolding layers of garments and small keepsakes; she spread them out on sheets on the floor around her, crying over certain things, nearly always the same things, looking again at pictures in velvet cases, unwrapping locks of hair and dried flowers, crying gently and easily as if tears were the only pleasure she had left.

If Maria and Miranda were very quiet, and touched nothing until it was offered, they might sit by her at these times, or come and go. There was a tacit understanding that her grief was strictly her own, and must not be noticed or mentioned. The little girls examined the objects, one by one, and did not find them, in themselves, impressive. Such dowdy little wreaths and necklaces, some of them made of pearly shells; such moth-eaten bunches of pink ostrich feathers for the hair; such clumsy big breast pins and bracelets of gold and colored enamel; such silly-looking combs, standing up on tall teeth capped with seed pearls and French paste. Miranda, without knowing why, felt melancholy. It seemed such a pity that these faded things, these yellowed long gloves

and misshapen satin slippers, these broad ribbons cracking where they were folded, should have been all those
vanished girls had to decorate themselves with. And
where were they now, those girls, and the boys in the
odd-looking collars? The young men seemed even more
unreal than the girls, with their high-buttoned coats,
their puffy neckties, their waxed mustaches, their waving
thick hair combed carefully over their foreheads. Who
could have taken them seriously, looking like that?

No, Maria and Miranda found it impossible to sym-
pathize with those young persons, sitting rather stiffly
before the camera, hopelessly out of fashion; but they
were drawn and held by the mysterious love of the living,
who remembered and cherished these dead. The visible
remains were nothing; they were dust, perishable as the
flesh; the features stamped on paper and metal were
nothing, but their living memory enchanted the little
girls. They listened, all ears and eager minds, picking
here and there among the floating ends of narrative,
patching together as well as they could fragments of tales
that were like bits of poetry or music, indeed were associated with the poetry they had heard or read, with
music, with the theater.

"Tell me again how Aunt Amy went away when she
was married." "She ran into the gray cold and stepped
into the carriage and turned and smiled with her face as
pale as death, and called out 'Good-by, good-by,' and
refused her cloak, and said, 'Give me a glass of wine.'
And none of us saw her alive again." "Why wouldn't
she wear her cloak, Cousin Cora?" "Because she was
not in love, my dear." Ruin hath taught me thus to
ruminate, that time will come and take my love away.
"Was she really beautiful, Uncle Bill?" "As an angel,

my child." There were golden-haired angels with long blue pleated skirts dancing around the throne of the Blessed Virgin. None of them resembled Aunt Amy in the least, nor the type of beauty they had been brought up to admire. There were points of beauty by which one was judged severely. First, a beauty must be tall; whatever color the eyes, the hair must be dark, the darker the better; the skin must be pale and smooth. Lightness and swiftness of movement were important points. A beauty must be a good dancer, superb on horseback, with a serene manner, an amiable gaiety tempered with dignity at all hours. Beautiful teeth and hands, of course, and over and above all this, some mysterious crown of enchantment that attracted and held the heart. It was all very exciting and discouraging.

Miranda persisted through her childhood in believing, in spite of her smallness, thinness, her little snubby nose saddled with freckles, her speckled gray eyes and habitual tantrums, that by some miracle she would grow into a tall, cream-colored brunette, like cousin Isabel; she decided always to wear a trailing white satin gown. Maria, born sensible, had no such illusions. "We are going to take after Mamma's family," she said. "It's no use, we are. We'll never be beautiful, we'll always have freckles. And *you*," she told Miranda, "haven't even a good disposition."

Miranda admitted both truth and justice in this unkindness, but still secretly believed that she would one day suddenly receive beauty, as by inheritance, riches laid suddenly in her hands through no deserts of her own. She believed for quite a while that she would one day be like Aunt Amy, not as she appeared in the photograph, but as she was remembered by those who had seen her.

When Cousin Isabel came out in her tight black riding habit, surrounded by young men, and mounted gracefully, drawing her horse up and around so that he pranced learnedly on one spot while the other riders sprang to their saddles in the same sedate flurry, Miranda's heart would close with such a keen dart of admiration, envy, vicarious pride it was almost painful; but there would always be an elder present to lay a cooling hand upon her emotions. "She rides almost as well as Amy, doesn't she? But Amy had the pure Spanish style, she could bring out paces in a horse no one else knew he had." Young namesake Amy, on her way to a dance, would swish through the hall in ruffled white taffeta, glimmering like a moth in the lamplight, carrying her elbows pointed backward stiffly as wings, sliding along as if she were on rollers, in the fashionable walk of her day. She was considered the best dancer at any party, and Maria, sniffing the wave of perfume that followed Amy, would clasp her hands and say, "Oh, I can't *wait* to be grown up." But the elders would agree that the first Amy had been lighter, more smooth and delicate in her waltzing; young Amy would never equal her, Cousin Molly Parrington, far past her youth, indeed she belonged to the generation before Aunt Amy, was a noted charmer. Men who had known her all her life still gathered about her; now that she was happily widowed for the second time there was no doubt that she would yet marry again. But Amy, said the elders, had the same high spirits and wit without boldness, and you really could not say that Molly had ever been discreet. She dyed her hair, and made jokes about it. She had a way of collecting the men around her in a corner, where she told them stories. She was an unnatural mother to her ugly daughter Eva, an old maid past forty while her mother was still the belle of the ball. "Born when I was fifteen, you remember," Molly would say shamelessly, looking an old beau straight in the eye, both of them remembering that he had been best man at her first wedding when she was past twenty-one. "Everyone said I was like a little girl with her doll."

Eva, shy and chinless, straining her upper lip over two enormous teeth, would sit in corners watching her mother. She looked hungry, her eyes were strained and tired. She wore her mother's old clothes, made over, and taught Latin in a Female Seminary. She believed in votes for women, and had traveled about, making speeches. When her mother was not present, Eva bloomed out a little, danced prettily, smiled, showing all her teeth, and was like a dry little plant set out in a gentle rain. Molly was merry about her ugly duckling. "It's lucky for me my daughter is an old maid. She's not so apt," said Molly naughtily, "to make a grandmother of me." Eva would blush as if she had been slapped.

Eva was a blot, no doubt about it, but the little girls felt she belonged to their everyday world of dull lessons to be learned, stiff shoes to be limbered up, scratchy flannels to be endured in cold weather, measles and disappointed expectations. Their Aunt Amy belonged to the world of poetry. The romance of Uncle Gabriel's long, unrewarded love for her, her early death, was such a story as one found in old books: unworldly books, but true, such as the Vita Nuova, the Sonnets of Shakespeare and the Wedding Song of Spenser; and poems by

Edgar Allan Poe. "Her tantalized spirit now blandly reposes, Forgetting or never regretting its roses. . . ." Their father read that to them, and said, "He was our greatest poet," and they knew that "our" meant he was Southern. Aunt Amy was real as the pictures in the old Holbein and Dürer books were real. The little girls lay flat on their stomachs and peered into a world of wonder, turning the shabby leaves that fell apart easily, not surprised at the sight of the Mother of God sitting on a hollow log nursing her Child; not doubting either Death or the Devil riding at the stirrups of the grim knight; not questioning the propriety of the stiffly dressed ladies of Sir Thomas More's household, seated in dignity on the floor, or seeming to be. They missed all the dog and pony shows, and lantern-slide entertainments, but their father took them to see "Hamlet," and "The Taming of the Shrew," and "Richard the Third," and a long sad play with Mary, Queen of Scots, in it. Miranda thought the magnificent lady in black velvet was truly the Queen of Scots, and was pained to learn that the real Queen had died long ago, and not at all on the night she, Miranda, had been present.

The little girls loved the theater, that world of personages taller than human beings, who swept upon the scene and invested it with their presences, their more than human voices, their gestures of gods and goddesses ruling a universe. But there was always a voice recalling other and greater occasions. Grandmother in her youth had heard Jenny Lind, and thought that Nellie Melba was much overrated. Father had seen Bernhardt, and Madame Modjeska was no sort of rival. When Paderewski played for the first time in their city, cousins came from all over the state and went from the grandmother's house to hear him. The little girls were left out of this great occasion. They shared the excitement of the going away, and shared the beautiful moment of return, when cousins stood about in groups, with coffee cups and glasses in their hands, talking in low voices, awed and happy. The little girls, struck with the sense of a great event, hung about in their nightgowns and listened, until someone noticed and hustled them away from the sweet nimbus of all that glory. One old gentleman, however, had heard Rubinstein frequently. He could not but feel that Rubinstein had reached the final height of musical interpretation, and, for him, Paderewski had been something of an anticlimax. The little girls heard him muttering on, holding up one hand, patting the air as if he were calling for silence. The others looked at him, and listened, without any disturbance of their grave tender mood. They had never heard Rubinstein; they had, one hour since, heard Paderewski, and why should anyone need to recall the past? Miranda, dragged away, half understanding the old gentleman, hated him. She felt that she too had heard Paderewski.

There was then a life beyond a life in this world, as well as in the next; such episodes confirmed for the little girls the nobility of human feeling, the divinity of man's vision of the unseen, the importance of life and death, the depths of the human heart, the romantic value of tragedy. Cousin Eva, on a certain visit, trying to interest them in the study of Latin, told them the story of John Wilkes Booth, who, handsomely garbed in a long black cloak, had leaped to the stage after assassinating President Lincoln. "Sic semper tyrannis," he had shouted superbly, in spite of his broken leg. The little girls never doubted that it had happened in just that way, and the moral seemed to be that one should always have Latin, or at least a good classical poetry quotation, to depend upon in great or desperate moments. Cousin Eva reminded them that no one, not even a good Southerner, could possibly approve of John Wilkes Booth's deed. It was murder, after all. They were to remember that. But Miranda, used to tragedy in books and in family legends—two great-uncles had committed suicide and a remote ancestress had gone mad for love—decided that, without the murder, there would have been no point to dressing up and leaping to the stage shouting in Latin. So how could she disapprove of the deed? It was a fine story. She knew a distantly related old gentleman who had been devoted to the art of Booth, had seen him in a great many plays, but not, alas, at his greatest moment. Miranda regretted this; it would have been so pleasant to have the assassination of Lincoln in the family.

Uncle Gabriel, who had loved Aunt Amy so desperately, still lived somewhere, though Miranda and Maria had never seen him. He had gone away, far away, after her death. He still owned racehorses, and ran them at famous tracks all over the country, and Miranda believed there could not possibly be a more brilliant career. He had married again, quite soon, and had written to Grandmother, asking her to accept his new wife as a daughter in place of Amy. Grandmother had written coldly, accepting, inviting them for a visit, but Uncle Gabriel had somehow never brought his bride home. Harry had visited them in New Orleans, and reported that the second wife was a very good-looking well-bred blonde girl who would undoubtedly be a good wife for Gabriel. Still, Uncle Gabriel's heart was broken. Faithfully once a year he wrote a letter to someone of the family, sending money for a wreath for Amy's grave. He had written a poem for her gravestone, and had come home, leaving his second wife in Atlanta, to see that it was carved properly. He could never account for having written this poem; he had certainly never tried to write a single rhyme since leaving school. Yet one day when he had been thinking about Amy, the verse occurred to him, out of the air. Maria and Miranda had seen it, printed in gold on a mourning card. Uncle Gabriel had sent a great number of them to be handed around among the family.

> "She lives again who suffered life,
> Then suffered death, and now set free
> A singing angel, she forgets
> The griefs of old mortality."

"Did she really sing?" Maria asked her father.

"Now what has that to do with it?" he asked. "It's a poem."

"I think it's very pretty," said Miranda, impressed. Uncle Gabriel was second cousin to her father and Aunt Amy. It brought poetry very near.

"Not so bad for tombstone poetry," said their father, "but it should be better."

Uncle Gabriel had waited five years to marry Aunt Amy. She had been ill, her chest was weak; she was engaged twice to other young men and broke her engagements for no reason; and she laughed at the advice of older and kinder-hearted persons who thought it very capricious of her not to return the devotion of such a handsome and romantic young man as Gabriel, her second cousin, too; it was not as if she would be marrying a stranger. Her coldness was said to have driven Gabriel to a wild life and even to drinking. His grandfather was wealthy and Gabriel was his favorite; they had quarreled over the racehorses, and Gabriel had shouted, "By God, I must have *something*." As if he had not everything already: youth, health, good looks, the prospect of riches, and a devoted family circle. His grandfather pointed out to him that he was little better than an ingrate, and showed signs of being a wastrel as well. Gabriel said, "You had racehorses, and made a good thing of them." "I never depended upon them for a livelihood, sir," said his grandfather.

Gabriel wrote letters about this and many other things to Amy from Saratoga and from Kentucky and from New Orleans, sending her presents, and flowers packed in ice, and telegrams. The presents were amusing, such as a huge cage full of small green lovebirds; or, as an ornament for her hair, a full-petaled enameled rose with paste dewdrops, with an enameled butterfly in brilliant colors suspended quivering on a gold wire about it; but the telegrams always frightened her mother, and the flowers, after a journey by train and then by stage into the country, were much the worse for wear. He would send roses when the rose garden at home was in full bloom. Amy could not help smiling over it, though her mother insisted it was touching and sweet of Gabriel. It must prove to Amy that she was always in his thoughts.

"That's no place for me," said Amy, but she had a way of speaking, a tone of voice, which made it impossible to discover what she meant by what she said. It was possible always that she might be serious. And she would not answer questions.

"Amy's wedding dress," said the grandmother, unfurling an immense cloak of dove-colored cut velvet, spreading beside it a silvery-gray watered-silk frock, and a small gray velvet toque with a dark red breast of feathers. Cousin Isabel, the beauty, sat with her. They talked to each other, and Miranda could listen if she chose.

"She would not wear white, nor a veil," said Grandmother. "I couldn't oppose her, for I had said my daughters should each have exactly the wedding dress they wanted. But Amy surprised me. 'Now what would I look like in white satin?' she asked. It's true she was pale, but she would have been angelic in it, and all of us told her so. 'I shall wear mourning if I like,' she said, 'it is *my* funeral, you know.' I reminded her that Lou and your mother had worn white with veils and it would please me to have my daughters all alike in that. Amy said, 'Lou and Isabel are not like me,' but I could not persuade her to explain what she meant. One day when she was ill she said, 'Mammy, I'm not long for this world,' but not as if she meant it. I told her, 'You might live as long as anyone, if only you will be sensible.' 'That's the whole trouble,' said Amy. 'I feel sorry for Gabriel,' she told me. 'He doesn't know what he's asking for.'

"I tried to tell her once more," said the grandmother, "that marriage and children would cure her of everything. 'All women of our family are delicate when they are young,' I said. 'Why, when I was your age no one expected me to live a year. It was called greensickness, and everybody knew there was only one cure.' 'If I live for a hundred years and turn green as grass,' said Amy, 'I still shan't want to marry Gabriel.' So I told her very seriously that if she truly felt that way she must never do it, and Gabriel must be told once for all, and sent away. He would get over it. 'I have told him, and I have sent him away,' said Amy. 'He just doesn't listen.' We both laughed at that, and I told her young girls found a hundred ways to deny they wished to be married, and a thousand more to test their power over men, but that she had more than enough of that, and now it was time for her to be entirely sincere and make her decision. As for me," said the grandmother, "I wished with all heart to marry your grandfather, and if he had not asked me, I should have asked him most certainly. Amy insisted that she could not imagine wanting to marry anybody. She would be, she said, a nice old maid like Eva Parrington. For even then it was pretty plain that Eva was an old maid, born. Harry said, 'Oh, Eva—Eva has no chin, that's her trouble. If you had no chin, Amy, you'd be in the same fix as Eva, no doubt.' Your Uncle Bill would say, 'When women haven't anything else, they'll take a vote for consolation. A pretty thin bed-fellow,' said your Uncle Bill. 'What I really need is a good dancing partner to guide me through life,' said Amy, 'that's the match I'm looking for.' It was no good trying to talk to her."

Her brothers remembered her tenderly as a sensible girl. After listening to their comments on her character and ways, Maria decided that they considered her sensible because she asked their advice about her appearance when she was going out to dance. If they found fault in any way, she would change her dress or her hair until they were pleased, and say, "You are an angel not to let your poor sister go out looking like a freak." But she would not listen to her father, nor to Gabriel. If Gabriel praised the frock she was wearing, she was apt to disappear and come back in another. He loved her long black hair, and once, lifting it up from her pillow when she was ill, said, "I love your hair, Amy, the most beautiful hair in the world." When he returned on his next visit, he found her with her hair cropped and curled close to her head. He was horrified, as if she had willfully mutilated herself. She would not let it grow again, not even to please her brothers. The photograph hanging on the wall was one she had made at that time to send to Gabriel, who sent it back without a word. This pleased her, and she framed the photograph. There was a thin inky scrawl low in one corner, "To dear brother Harry, who likes my hair cut."

This was a mischievous reference to a very grave scandal. The little girls used to look at their father, and wonder what would have happened if he had really hit the young man he shot at. The young man was believed to have kissed Aunt Amy, when she was not in the least engaged to him. Uncle Gabriel was supposed to have had a duel with the young man, but Father had got there first. He was a pleasant, everyday sort of father, who held his daughters on his knee if they were prettily dressed and well behaved, and pushed them away if they had not freshly combed hair and nicely scrubbed fingernails. "Go away, you're disgusting," he would say, in a matter-of-fact voice. He noticed if their stocking seams were crooked. He caused them to brush their teeth with a revolting mixture of prepared chalk, powdered charcoal and salt. When they behaved stupidly he could not endure the sight of them. They understood dimly that all this was for their own future good; and when they were snivelly with colds, he prescribed delicious hot toddy for them, and saw that it was given them. He was always hoping they might not grow up to be so silly as they seemed to him at any given moment, and he had a disconcerting way of inquiring, "How do you *know*?" when they forgot and made dogmatic statements in his presence. It always came out embarrassingly that they did not know at all, but were repeating something they had heard. This made conversation with him difficult for he laid traps and they fell into them, but it became important to them that their father should not believe them to be fools. Well, this very father had gone to Mexico once and stayed there for nearly a year, because he had shot a man with whom Aunt Amy had flirted at a dance. It had been very wrong of him, because he should have challenged the man to a duel, as Uncle Gabriel had done. Instead, he just took a shot at him, and this was the lowest sort of manners. It had caused great disturbance in the whole community and had almost broken up the affair between Aunt Amy and Uncle Gabriel for good. Uncle Gabriel insisted that the young man had kissed Aunt Amy, and Aunt Amy insisted that the young man had merely paid her a compliment on her hair.

During the Mardi Gras holidays there was to be a big gay fancy-dress ball. Harry was going as a bull-fighter because his sweetheart, Mariana, had a new black lace mantilla and high comb from Mexico. Maria and Miranda had seen a photograph of their mother in this dress, her lovely face without a trace of coquetry looking gravely out from under a tremendous fall of lace from the peak of the comb, a rose tucked firmly over her ear. Amy copied her costume from a small Dresden china shepherdess which stood on the mantelpiece in the parlor; a careful copy with ribboned hat, gilded crook, very low-laced bodice, short basket skirts, green slippers and all. She wore it with a black half-mask, but it was no disguise. "You would have known it was Amy at any distance," said Father. Gabriel, six feet three in height as he was, had got himself up to match, and a spectacle he provided in pale blue satin knee breeches and a blond curled wig with a hair ribbon. "He felt a fool, and he looked like one," said Uncle Bill, "and he behaved like one before the evening was over."

Everything went beautifully until the party gathered downstairs to leave for the ball. Amy's father—he must have been born a grandfather, thought Miranda—gave one glance at his daughter, her white ankles shining, bosom deeply exposed, two round spots of paint on her cheeks, and fell into a frenzy of outraged propriety. "It's disgraceful," he pronounced, loudly. "No daughter of mine is going to show herself in such a rig-out. It's bawdy," he thundered. "Bawdy!"

Amy had taken off her mask to smile at him. "Why, Papa," she said very sweetly, "what's wrong with it? Look on the mantelpiece. She's been there all along, and you were never shocked before."

"There's all the difference in the world," said her father, "all the difference, young lady, and you know it. You go upstairs this minute and pin up that waist in front and let down those skirts to a decent length before you leave this house. *And wash your face!*"

"I see nothing wrong with it," said Amy's mother, firmly, "and you shouldn't use such language before innocent young girls." She and Amy sat down with several females of the household to help, and they made short work of the business. In ten minutes Amy returned, face clean, bodice filled in with lace, shepherdess skirt modestly sweeping the carpet behind her.

When Amy appeared from the dressing room for her first dance with Gabriel, the lace was gone from her bodice, her skirts were tucked up more daringly than before, and the spots on her cheeks were like pomegranates. "Now Gabriel, tell me truly, wouldn't it have been a pity to spoil my costume?" Gabriel, delighted that she had asked his opinion, declared it was perfect. They agreed with kindly tolerance that old people were often tiresome, but one need not upset them by open disobedience: their youth was gone, what had they to live for?

Harry, dancing with Mariana who swung a heavy tram around her expertly at every turn of the waltz, began to be uneasy about his sister Amy. She was entirely too popular. He saw young men make beelines across the floor, eyes fixed on those white silk ankles. Some of the young men he did not know at all, others he knew too well and could not approve of for his sister Amy. Gabriel, unhappy in his lyric satin and wig, stood about holding his ribboned crook as though it had sprouted thorns. He hardly danced at all with Amy, he did not enjoy dancing with anyone else, and he was having a thoroughly wretched time of it.

There appeared late, alone, got up as Jean Lafitte, a young Creole gentleman who had, two years before, been for a time engaged to Amy. He came straight to her, with the manner of a happy lover, and said, clearly enough for everyone nearby to hear him, "I only came because I knew you were to be here. I only want to dance with you and I shall go again." Amy, with a face of delight, cried out, "Raymond!" as if to a lover. She had danced with him four times, and had then disappeared from the floor on his arm.

Harry and Mariana, in conventional disguise of romance, irreproachably betrothed, safe in their happiness, were waltzing slowly to their favorite song, the melancholy farewell of the Moorish King on leaving Granada. They sang in whispers to each other, in their uncertain Spanish, a song of love and parting and that sword's point of grief that makes the heart tender towards all other lost and disinherited creatures: Oh, mansion of love, my earthly paradise . . . that I shall see no more . . . whither flies the poor swallow, weary and homeless, seeking for shelter where no shelter is? I too am far from home without the power to fly. . . . Come to my heart, sweet bird, beloved pilgrim, build your nest near my bed, let me listen to your song, and weep for my lost land of joy. . . .

Into this bliss broke Gabriel. He had thrown away his shepherd's crook and he was carrying his wig. He wanted to speak to Harry at once, and before Mariana knew what was happening she was sitting beside her mother and the two excited young men were gone. Waiting, disturbed and displeased, she smiled at Amy who waltzed past with a young man in Devil costume, including ill-fitting scarlet cloven hoofs. Almost at once, Harry and Gabriel came back, with serious faces, and Harry darted on the dance floor, returning with Amy. The girls and the chaperones were asked to come at once, they must be taken home. It was all mysterious and sudden, and Harry said to Mariana, "I will tell you what is happening, but not now—"

The grandmother remembered of this disgraceful affair only that Gabriel brought Amy home alone and that

Harry came in somewhat later. The other members of
the party straggled in at various hours, and the story
came out piecemeal. Amy was silent and, her mother
discovered later, burning with fever. "I saw at once that
something was very wrong. 'What has happened, Amy?'
'Oh, Harry goes about shooting at people at a party,'
she said, sitting down as if she were exhausted. 'It was
on your account, Amy,' said Gabriel. 'Oh, no, it was
not,' said Amy. 'Don't believe him, Mammy.' So I said,
'Now enough of this. Tell me what happened, Amy.
And Amy said, 'Mammy, this is it. Raymond came in,
and you know I like Raymond, and he is a good dancer.
So we danced together, too much, maybe. We went on
the gallery for a breath of air, and stood there. He said,
"How well your hair looks. I like this new shingled
style." ' She glanced at Gabriel. 'And then another
young man came out and said, "I've been looking every-
where. This is our dance, isn't it?" And I went in to
dance. And now it seems that Gabriel went out at once
and challenged Raymond to a duel about something or
other, but Harry doesn't wait for that. Raymond had
already gone out to have his horse brought, I suppose
one doesn't duel in fancy dress,' she said, looking at
Gabriel, who fairly shriveled in his blue satin shepherd's
costume, 'and Harry simply went out and shot at him.
I don't think that was fair,' said Amy."

Her mother agreed that indeed it was not fair; it was
not even decent, and she could not imagine what her son
Harry thought he was doing. "It isn't much of a way to
defend your sister's honor," she said to him afterward.
"I didn't want Gabriel to go fighting duels," said Harry.
"That wouldn't have helped much, either."

Gabriel had stood before Amy, leaning over, asking

once more the question he had apparently been asking her all the way home. "Did he kiss you, Amy?"

Amy took off her shepherdess hat and pushed her hair back. "Maybe he did," she answered, "and maybe I wished him to."

"Amy, you must not say such things," said her mother. "Answer Gabriel's question."

"He hasn't the right to ask it," said Amy, but without anger.

"Do you love him, Amy?" asked Gabriel, the sweat standing out on his forehead.

"It doesn't matter," answered Amy, leaning back in her chair.

"Oh, it does matter; it matters terribly," said Gabriel. "You must answer me now." He took both of her hands and tried to hold them. She drew her hands away firmly and steadily so that he had to let go.

"Let her alone, Gabriel," said Amy's mother. "You'd better go now. We are all tired. Let's talk about it to-morrow."

She helped Amy to undress, noticing the changed bodice and the shortened skirt. "You shouldn't have done that, Amy. That was not wise of you. It was better the other way."

Amy said, "Mammy, I'm sick of this world. I don't like anything in it. It's so *dull*," she said, and for a moment she looked as if she might weep. She had never been tearful, even as a child, and her mother was alarmed. It was then she discovered that Amy had fever.

"Gabriel is dull, Mother—he sulks," she said. "I could see him sulking every time I passed. It spoils things," she said. "Oh, I want to go to sleep."

Her mother sat looking at her and wondering how it

had happened she had brought such a beautiful child into the world. "Her face," said her mother, "was angelic in sleep."

Some time during that fevered night, the projected duel between Gabriel and Raymond was halted by the offices of friends on both sides. There remained the open question of Harry's impulsive shot, which was not so easily settled. Raymond seemed vindictive about that, it was possible he might choose to make trouble. Harry, taking the advice of Gabriel, his brothers and friends, decided that the best way to avoid further scandal was for him to disappear for a while. This being decided upon, the young men returned about daybreak, saddled Harry's best horse and helped him pack a few things; accompanied by Gabriel and Bill, Harry set out for the border, feeling rather gay and adventurous.

Amy, being wakened by the stirring in the house, found out the plan. Five minutes after they were gone, she came down in her riding dress, had her own horse saddled, and struck out after them. She rode almost every morning; before her parents had time to be uneasy over her prolonged absence, they found her note.

What had threatened to be a tragedy became a rowdy lark. Amy rode to the border, kissed her brother Harry good-by, and rode back again with Bill and Gabriel. It was a three days' journey, and when they arrived Amy had to be lifted from the saddle. She was really ill by now, but in the gayest of humors. Her mother and father had been prepared to be severe with her, but, at sight of her, their feelings changed. They turned on Bill and Gabriel. "Why did you let her do this?" they asked.

"You know we could not stop her," said Gabriel helplessly, "and she did enjoy herself so much!"

Amy laughed. "Mammy, it was splendid, the most delightful trip I ever had. And if I am to be the heroine of this novel, why shouldn't I make the most of it?"

The scandal, Maria and Miranda gathered, had been pretty terrible. Amy simply took to bed and stayed there, and Harry had skipped out blithely to wait until the little affair blew over. The rest of the family had to receive visitors, write letters, go to church, return calls, and bear the whole brunt, as they expressed it. They sat in the twilight of scandal in their little world, holding themselves very rigidly, in a shared tension as if all their nerves began at a common center. This center had received a blow, and family nerves shuddered, even into the farthest reaches of Kentucky. From whence in due time great-great-aunt Sally Rhea addressed a letter to *Mifs Amy Rhea*. In deep brown ink like dried blood, in a spidery hand adept at archaic symbols and abbreviations, great-great-aunt Sally informed Amy that she was fairly convinced that this calamity was only the forerunner of a series shortly to be visited by the Almighty God upon a race already condemned through its own wickedness, a warning that man's time was short, and that they must all prepare for the end of the world. For herself, she had long expected it, she was entirely resigned to the prospect of meeting her Maker; and Amy, no less than her wicked brother Harry, must likewise place herself in God's hands and prepare for the worst. "*Oh, my dear unfortunate young relative*," twittered great-great-aunt Sally, "*we must in our Extremty join hands and appr before ye Dread Throne of Jdgmnt a United Fmly, if One is Mssg from ye Flock, what will Jesus say?*"

Great-great-aunt Sally's religious career had become

comic legend. She had forsaken her Catholic rearing for a young man whose family were Cumberland Presbyterians. Unable to accept their opinions, however, she was converted to the Hard-Shell Baptists, a sect as loathsome to her husband's family as the Catholic could possibly be. She had spent a life of vicious self-indulgent martyrdom to her faith; as Harry commented: "Religion put claws on Aunt Sally and gave her a post to whet them on." She had out-argued, out-fought, and outlived her entire generation, but she did not miss them. She bedeviled the second generation without ceasing, and was beginning hungrily on the third.

Amy, reading this letter, broke into her gay full laugh that always caused everyone around her to laugh too, even before they knew why, and her small green lovebirds in their cage turned and eyed her solemnly. "Imagine drawing a pew in heaven beside Aunt Sally," she said. "What a prospect."

"Don't laugh too soon," said her father. "Heaven was made to order for Aunt Sally. She'll be on her own territory there."

"For my sins," said Amy, "I must go to heaven with Aunt Sally."

During the uncomfortable time of Harry's absence, Amy went on refusing to marry Gabriel. Her mother could hear their voices going on in their endless colloquy, during many long days. One afternoon Gabriel came out, looking very sober and discouraged. He stood looking down at Amy's mother as she sat sewing, and said, "I think it is all over, I believe now that Amy will never have me." The grandmother always said afterward, "Never have I pitied anyone as I did poor Gabriel at that moment. But I told him, very firmly, 'Let her alone, then, she is ill.' " So Gabriel left, and Amy had no word from him for more than a month.

The day after Gabriel was gone, Amy rose looking extremely well, went hunting with her brothers Bill and Stephen, bought a velvet wrap, had her hair shingled and curled again, and wrote long letters to Harry, who was having a most enjoyable exile in Mexico City.

After dancing all night three times in one week, she woke one morning in a hemorrhage. She seemed frightened and asked for the doctor, promising to do whatever he advised. She was quiet for a few days, reading. She asked for Gabriel. No one knew where he was. "You should write him a letter; his mother will send it on." "Oh, no," she said. "I miss him coming in with his sour face. Letters are no good."

Gabriel did come in, only a few days later, with a very sour face and unpleasant news. His grandfather had died, after a day's illness. On his death bed, in the name of God, being of a sound and disposing mind, he had cut off his favorite grandchild Gabriel with one dollar. "In the name of God, Amy," said Gabriel, "the old devil has ruined me in one sentence."

It was the conduct of his immediate family in the matter that had embittered him, he said. They could hardly conceal their satisfaction. They had known and envied Gabriel's quite just, well-founded expectations. Not one of them offered to make any private settlement. No one even thought of repairing this last-minute act of senile vengeance. Privately they blessed their luck. "I have been cut off with a dollar," said Gabriel, "and they are all glad of it. I think they feel somehow that this justifies every criticism they ever made against me. They were right about me all along. I am a worthless poor relation,' said Gabriel. "My God, I wish you could see them."

Amy said, "I wonder how you will ever support a wife, now."

Gabriel said, "Oh, it isn't so bad as that. If you would Amy—"

Amy said, "Gabriel, if we get married now there'll be just time to be in New Orleans for Mardi Gras. If we wait until after Lent, it may be too late."

"Why, Amy," said Gabriel, "how could it ever be too late?"

"You might change your mind," said Amy. "You know how fickle you are."

There were two letters in the grandmother's many packets of letters that Maria and Miranda read after they were grown. One of them was from Amy. It was dated ten days after her marriage.

"Dear Mammy, New Orleans hasn't changed as much as I have since we saw each other last. I am now a staid old married woman, and Gabriel is very devoted and kind. Footlights won a race for us yesterday, she was the favorite, and it was wonderful. I go to the races every day, and our horses are doing splendidly; I had my choice of Erin Go Bragh or Miss Lucy, and I chose Miss Lucy. She is mine now, she runs like a streak. Gabriel says I made a mistake, Erin Go Bragh will stay better. I think Miss Lucy will stay my time.

"We are having a lovely visit. I'm going to put on a domino and take to the streets with Gabriel sometime during Mardi Gras. I'm tired of watching the show from a balcony. Gabriel says it isn't safe. He says he'll take me if I insist, but I doubt it. Mammy, he's very nice. Don't worry about me. I have a beautiful black-and-rose-colored velvet gown for the Proteus Ball. Madame, my new mother-in-law, wanted to know if it wasn't a little dashing. I told her I hoped so or I had been cheated. It is fitted perfectly smooth in the bodice, very low in the shoulders—Papa would not approve—and the skirt is looped with wide silver ribbons between the waist and knees in front, and then it surges around and is looped enormously in the back, with a train just one yard long. I now have an eighteen-inch waist, thanks to Madame Duré. I expect to be so dashing that my mother-in-law will have an attack. She has them quite often. Gabriel sends love. Please take good care of Graylie and Fiddler. I want to ride them again when I come home. We're going to Saratoga, I don't know just when. Give everybody my dear dear love. It rains all the time here, of course. . . .

"P.S. Mammy, as soon as I get a minute to myself, I'm going to be terribly homesick. Good-by, my darling Mammy."

The other was from Amy's nurse, dated six weeks after Amy's marriage.

"I cut off the lock of hair because I was sure you would like to have it. And I do not want you to think I was careless, leaving her medicine where she could get it, the doctor has written and explained. It would not have done her any harm except that her heart was weak. She did not know how much she was taking, often she said to me, one more of those little capsules wouldn't do any harm, and so I told her to be careful and not take anything except what I gave her. She begged me for them sometimes but I would not give her more than the doctor said. I slept during the night because she did not seem to be so sick as all that and the doctor did not order me to sit up with her. Please accept my regrets for your great loss and please do not think that anybody was careless with your dear daughter. She suffered a great deal and now she is at rest. She could not get well but she might have lived longer. Yours respectfully. . . ."

The letters and all the strange keepsakes were packed away and forgotten for a great many years. They seemed to have no place in the world.

PART II: 1904

During vacation on their grandmother's farm, Maria and Miranda, who read as naturally and constantly as ponies crop grass, and with much the same kind of pleasure, had by some happy chance laid hold of some forbidden reading matter, brought in and left there with missionary intent, no doubt, by some Protestant cousin. It fell into the right hands if enjoyment had been its end. The reading matter was printed in poor type on spongy paper, and was ornamented with smudgy illustrations all the more exciting to the little girls because they could not make head or tail of them. The stories were about beautiful but unlucky maidens, who for mysterious reasons had been trapped by nuns and priests in dire collusion; they were then "immured" in convents, where they were forced to take the veil—an appalling rite during which the victims shrieked dreadfully—and condemned forever after to most uncomfortable and disorderly existences.

They seemed to divide their time between lying chained in dark cells and assisting other nuns to bury throttled infants under stones in moldering rat-infested dungeons.

Immured! It was the word Maria and Miranda had been needing all along to describe their condition at the Convent of the Child Jesus, in New Orleans, where they spent the long winters trying to avoid an education. There were no dungeons at the Child Jesus, and this was only one of numerous marked differences between convent life as Maria and Miranda knew it and the thrilling paper-backed version. It was no good at all trying to fit the stories to life, and they did not even try. They had long since learned to draw the lines between life, which was real and earnest, and the grave was not its goal; poetry, which was true but not real; and stories, or forbidden reading matter, in which things happened as nowhere else, with the most sublime irrelevance and unlikelihood, and one need not turn a hair, because there was not a word of truth in them.

It was true the little girls were hedged and confined, but in a large garden with trees and a grotto; they were locked at night into a long cold dormitory, with all the windows open, and a sister sleeping at either end. Their beds were curtained with muslin, and small night-lamps were so arranged that the sisters could see through the curtains, but the children could not see the sisters. Miranda wondered if they ever slept, or did they sit there all night quietly watching the sleepers through the muslin? She tried to work up a little sinister thrill about this, but she found it impossible to care much what either of the sisters did. They were very dull good-natured women who managed to make the whole dormitory seem dull. All days and all things in the Convent of the Child Jesus were dull in fact, and Maria and Miranda lived for Saturdays.

No one had even hinted that they should become nuns. On the contrary Miranda felt that the discouraging attitude of Sister Claude and Sister Austin and Sister Ursula towards her expressed ambition to be a nun barely veiled a deeply critical knowledge of her spiritual deficiencies. Still Maria and Miranda had got a fine new word out of their summer reading, and they referred to themselves as "immured." It gave a romantic glint to what was otherwise a very dull life for them, except for blessed Saturday afternoons during the racing season.

If the nuns were able to assure the family that the deportment and scholastic achievements of Maria and Miranda were at least passable, some cousin or other always showed up smiling, in holiday mood, to take them to the races, where they were given a dollar each to bet on any horse they chose. There were black Saturdays now and then, when Maria and Miranda sat ready, hats in hand, curly hair plastered down and slicked behind their ears, their stiffly pleated navy-blue skirts spread out around them, waiting with their hearts going down slowly into their high-topped laced-up black shoes. They never put on their hats until the last minute, for somehow it would have been too horrible to have their hats on, when, after all, Cousin Henry and Cousin Isabel, or Uncle George and Aunt Polly, were not coming to take them to the races. When no one appeared, and Saturday came and went a sickening waste, they were then given to understand that it was a punishment for bad marks during the week. They never knew until it was too late to avoid the disappointment. It was very wearing.

One Saturday they were sent down to wait in the visitors' parlor, and there was their father. He had come all the way from Texas to see them. They leaped at sight of him, and then stopped short, suspiciously. Was he going to take them to the races? If so, they were happy to see him.

"Hello," said father, kissing their cheeks. "Have you been good girls? Your Uncle Gabriel is running a mare at the Crescent City today, so we'll all go and bet on her. Would you like that?"

Maria put on her hat without a word, but Miranda stood and addressed her father sternly. She had suffered many doubts about this day. "*Why* didn't you send word yesterday? I could have been looking forward all this time."

"We didn't know," said father, in his easiest paternal manner, "that you were going to deserve it. Remember Saturday before last?"

Miranda hung her head and put on her hat, with the round elastic under the chin. She remembered too well. She had, in midweek, given way to despair over her arithmetic and had fallen flat on her face on the classroom floor, refusing to rise until she was carried out. The rest of the week had been a series of novel deprivations, and Saturday a day of mourning; secret mourning, for if one mourned too noisily, it simply meant another bad mark against deportment.

"Never mind," said father, as if it were the smallest possible matter, "today you're going. Come along now. We've barely time."

These expeditions were all joy, every time, from the moment they stepped into a closed one-horse cab, a treat in itself with its dark, thick upholstery, soaked with strange perfumes and tobacco smoke, until the thrilling moment when they walked into a restaurant under big lights and were given dinner with things to eat they never had at home, much less at the convent. They felt worldly and grown up, each with her glass of water colored pink with claret.

The great crowd was always exciting as if they had never seen it before, with the beautiful, incredibly dressed ladies, all plumes and flowers and paint, and the elegant gentlemen with yellow gloves. The bands played in turn with thundering drums and brasses, and now and then a wild beautiful horse would career around the track with a tiny, monkey-shaped boy on his back, limbering up for his race.

Miranda had a secret personal interest in all this which she knew better than to confide to anyone, even Maria. Least of all to Maria. In ten minutes the whole family would have known. She had lately decided to be a jockey when she grew up. Her father had said one day that she was going to be a little thing all her life, she would never be tall; and this meant, of course, that she would never be a beauty like Aunt Amy, or Cousin Isabel. Her hope of being a beauty died hard, until the notion of being a jockey came suddenly and filled all her thoughts. Quietly, blissfully, at night before she slept, and too often in the daytime when she should have been studying, she planned her career as jockey. It was dim in detail, but brilliant at the right distance. It seemed too silly to be worried about arithmetic at all, when what she needed for her future was to ride better—much better. "You ought to be ashamed of yourself," said father, after watching her gallop full tilt down the lane at the farm, on Trixie, the mustang mare. "I can see the sun, moon and stars between you and the saddle every jump." Spanish style meant that one sat close to the saddle, and did all kinds of things with the knees and reins. Jockeys bounced lightly, their knees almost level with the horse's back, rising and falling like a rubber ball. Miranda felt she could do that easily. Yes, she would be a jockey, like Tod Sloan, winning every other race at least. Meantime, while she was training, she would keep it a secret, and one day she would ride out, bouncing lightly, with the other jockeys, and win a great race, and surprise everybody, her family most of all.

On that particular Saturday, her idol, the great Tod Sloan, was riding, and he won two races. Miranda longed to bet her dollar on Tod Sloan, but father said, "Not now, honey. Today you must bet on Uncle Gabriel's horse. Save your dollar for the fourth race, and put it on Miss Lucy. You've got a hundred to one shot. Think if she wins."

Miranda knew well enough that a hundred to one shot was no bet at all. She sulked, the crumpled dollar in her hand grew damp and warm. She could have won three dollars already on Tod Sloan. Maria said virtuously, "It wouldn't be nice not to bet on Uncle Gabriel. That way, we keep the money in the family." Miranda put out her under lip at her sister. Maria was too prissy for words. She wrinkled her nose back at Miranda.

They had just turned their dollar over to the bookmaker for the fourth race when a vast bulging man with a red face and immense tan ragged mustaches fading into gray hailed them from a lower level of the grandstand, over the heads of the crowd, "Hey, there, Harry?" Father said, "Bless my soul, there's Gabriel." He motioned to the man, who came pushing his way heavily up the shallow steps. Maria and Miranda stared, first at him, then at each other. "Can that be our Uncle Gabriel?" their eyes asked. "Is that Aunt Amy's handsome romantic beau? Is that the man who wrote the poem about our Aunt Amy?" Oh, what did grown-up people *mean* when they talked, anyway?

He was a shabby fat man with bloodshot blue eyes, sad beaten eyes, and a big melancholy laugh, like a groan. He towered over them shouting to their father, "Well, for God's sake, Harry, it's been a coon's age. You ought to come out and look 'em over. You look just like yourself, Harry, how are you?"

The band struck up "Over the River" and Uncle Gabriel shouted louder. "Come on, let's get out of this. What are you doing up here with the pikers?"

"Can't," shouted Father. "Brought my little girls. Here they are."

Uncle Gabriel's bleared eyes beamed blindly upon them. "Fine looking set, Harry," he bellowed, "pretty as pictures, how old are they?"

"Ten and fourteen now," said Father; "awkward ages. Nest of vipers," he boasted, "perfect batch of serpent's teeth. Can't do a thing with 'em." He fluffed up Miranda's hair, pretending to tousle it.

"Pretty as pictures," bawled Uncle Gabriel, "but rolled into one they don't come up to Amy, do they?"

"No, they don't," admitted their father at the top of his voice, "but they're only half-baked." *Over the river, over the river,* moaned the band, *my sweetheart's waiting for me.*

"I've got to get back now," yelled Uncle Gabriel. The little girls felt quite deaf and confused. "Got the Goddamnedest jockey in the world, Harry, just my luck.

Ought to tie him on. Fell off Fiddler yesterday, just plain fell off on his tail—Remember Amy's mare, Miss Lucy? Well, this is her namesake, Miss Lucy IV. None of 'em ever came up to the first one, though. Stay right where you are, I'll be back."

Maria spoke up boldly. "Uncle Gabriel, tell Miss Lucy we're betting on her." Uncle Gabriel bent down and it looked as if there were tears in his swollen eyes. "God bless your sweet heart," he bellowed, "I'll tell her." He plunged down through the crowd again, his fat back bowed slightly in his loose clothes, his thick neck rolling over his collar.

Miranda and Maria, disheartened by the odds, by their first sight of their romantic Uncle Gabriel, whose language was so coarse, sat listlessly without watching, their chances missed, their dollars gone, their hearts sore. They didn't even move until their father leaned over and hauled them up. "Watch your horse," he said, in a quick warning voice, "watch Miss Lucy come home."

They stood up, scrambled to their feet on the bench, every vein in them suddenly beating so violently they could hardly focus their eyes, and saw a thin little mahogany-colored streak flash by the judges' stand, only a neck ahead, but their Miss Lucy, oh, their darling, their lovely—oh, Miss Lucy, their Uncle Gabriel's Miss Lucy, had won, had won. They leaped up and down screaming and clapping their hands, their hats falling back on their shoulders, their hair flying wild. *Whoa, you heifer*, squalled the band with snorting brasses, and the crowd broke into a long roar like the falling of the walls of Jericho.

The little girls sat down, feeling quite dizzy, while their father tried to pull their hats straight, and taking out his handkerchief held it to Miranda's face, saying very gently, "Here, blow your nose," and he dried her eyes while he was about it. He stood up then and shook them out of their daze. He was smiling with deep laughing wrinkles around his eyes, and spoke to them as if they were grown young ladies he was squiring around.

"Let's go out and pay our respects to Miss Lucy," he said. "She's the star of the day."

The horses were coming in, looking as if their hides had been drenched and rubbed with soap, their ribs heaving, their nostrils flaring and closing. The jockeys sat bowed and relaxed, their faces calm, moving a little at the waist with the movement of their horses. Miranda noted this for future use; that was the way you came in from a race, easy and quiet, whether you had won or lost. Miss Lucy came last, and a little handful of winners applauded her and cheered the jockey. He smiled and lifted his whip, his eyes and shriveled brown face perfectly serene. Miss Lucy was bleeding at the nose, two thick red rivulets were stiffening her tender mouth and chin, the round velvet chin that Miranda thought the nicest kind of chin in the world. Her eyes were wild and her knees were trembling, and she snored when she drew her breath.

Miranda stood staring. That was winning, too. Her heart clinched tight; that was winning, for Miss Lucy. So instantly and completely did her heart reject that victory, she did not know when it happened, but she hated it, and was ashamed that she had screamed and shed tears for joy when Miss Lucy, with her bloodied nose and bursting heart had gone past the judges' stand a neck ahead. She felt empty and sick and held to her father's hand so hard that he shook her off a little impatiently and said, "What is the matter with you? Don't be so fidgety."

Uncle Gabriel was standing there waiting, and he was completely drunk. He watched the mare go in, then leaned against the fence with its white-washed posts and sobbed openly. "She's got the nosebleed, Harry," he said. "Had it since yesterday. We thought we had her all fixed up. But she did it, all right. She's got a heart like a lion. I'm going to breed her, Harry. Her heart's worth a million dollars, by itself, God bless her." Tears ran over his brick-colored face and into his straggling mustaches. "If anything happens to her now I'll blow my brains out. She's my last hope. She saved my life. I've had a run," he said, groaning into a large handkerchief and mopping his face all over, "I've had a run of luck that would break a brass billy goat. God, Harry, let's go somewhere and have a drink."

"I must get the children back to school first, Gabriel," said their father, taking each by a hand.

"No, no, don't go yet," said Uncle Gabriel desperately. "Wait here a minute, I want to see the vet and take a look at Miss Lucy, and I'll be right back. Don't go, Harry, for God's sake. I want to talk to you a few minutes."

Maria and Miranda, watching Uncle Gabriel's lumbering, unsteady back, were thinking that this was the first time they had ever seen a man that they knew to be drunk. They had seen pictures and read descriptions, and had heard descriptions, so they recognized the symptoms at once. Miranda felt it was an important moment in a great many ways.

"Uncle Gabriel's a drunkard, isn't he?" she asked her father, rather proudly.

"Hush, don't say such things," said father, with a heavy frown, "or I'll never bring you here again." He looked worried and unhappy, and, above all, undecided. The little girls stood stiff with resentment against such obvious injustice. They loosed their hands from his and moved away coldly, standing together in silence. Their father did not notice, watching the place where Uncle Gabriel had disappeared. In a few minutes he came back, still wiping his face, as if there were cobwebs on it, carrying his big black hat. He waved at them from a short distance, calling out in a cheerful way, "She's going to be all right, Harry. It's stopped now. Lord, this will be good news for Miss Honey. Come on, Harry, let's all go home and tell Miss Honey. She deserves some good news."

Father said, "I'd better take the children back to school first, then we'll go."

"No, no," said Uncle Gabriel, fondly. "I want her to see the girls. She'll be tickled pink to see them, Harry. Bring 'em along."

"Is it another race horse we're going to see?" whispered Miranda in her sister's ear.

"Don't be silly," said Maria. "It's Uncle Gabriel's second wife."

"Let's find a cab, Harry," said Uncle Gabriel, "and take your little girls out to cheer up Miss Honey. Both of 'em rolled into one look a lot like Amy, I swear they do. I want Miss Honey to see them. She's always liked our family, Harry, though of course she's not what you'd call an expansive kind of woman."

Maria and Miranda sat facing the driver, and Uncle Gabriel squeezed himself in facing them beside their father. The air became at once bitter and sour with his breathing. He looked sad and poor. His necktie was on crooked and his shirt was rumpled. Father said, "You're going to see Uncle Gabriel's second wife, children," exactly if they had not heard everything; and to Gabriel, "How *is* your wife nowadays? It must be twenty years since I saw her last."

"She's pretty gloomy, and that's a fact," said Uncle Gabriel. "She's been pretty gloomy for years now, and nothing seems to shake her out of it. She never did care for horses, Harry, if you remember; she hasn't been near the track three times since we were married. When I think how Amy wouldn't have missed a race for anything . . . She's very different from Amy, Harry, a very different kind of woman. As fine a woman as ever lived in her own way, but she hates change and moving around, and she just lives in the boy."

"Where is Gabe now?" asked father.

"Finishing college," said Uncle Gabriel; "a smart boy, but awfully like his mother. Awfully like," he said, in a melancholy way. "She hates being away from him. Just wants to sit down in the same town and wait for him to get through with his education. Well, I'm sorry it can't be done if that's what she wants, but God Almighty—And this last run of luck has about got her down. I hope you'll be able to cheer her up a little, Harry, she needs it."

The little girls sat watching the streets grow duller and dingier and narrower, and at last the shabbier and shab- bier white people gave way to dressed-up Negroes, and then to shabby Negroes, and after a long way the cab stopped before a desolate-looking little hotel in Elysian Fields. Their father helped Maria and Miranda out, told the cabman to wait, and they followed Uncle Gabriel through a dirty damp-smelling patio, down a long gas-lighted hall full of a terrible smell, Miranda couldn't decide what it was made of but it had a bitter taste even, and up a long staircase with a ragged carpet. Uncle Gabriel pushed open a door without warning, saying, "Come in, here we are."

A tall pale-faced woman with faded straw-colored hair and pink-rimmed eyelids rose suddenly from a squeaking rocking chair. She wore a stiff blue-and-white-striped shirtwaist and a stiff black skirt of some hard shiny material. Her large knuckled hands rose to her round, neat pompadour at sight of her visitors.

"Honey," said Uncle Gabriel, with large false heartiness, "you'll never guess who's come to see you." He gave her a clumsy hug. Her face did not change and her eyes rested steadily on the three strangers. "Amy's brother Harry, Honey, you remember, don't you?"

"Of course," said Miss Honey, putting out her hand straight as a paddle, "of course I remember you, Harry." She did not smile.

"And Amy's two little nieces," went on Uncle Gabriel, bringing them forward. They put out their hands limply, and Miss Honey gave each one a slight flip and dropped it. "And we've got good news for you," went on Uncle Gabriel, trying to bolster up the painful situation. "Miss Lucy stepped out and showed 'em today, Honey. We're rich again, old girl, cheer up."

Miss Honey turned her long, despairing face towards her visitors. "Sit down," she said with a heavy sigh, seating herself and motioning towards various rickety chairs. There was a big lumpy bed, with a grayish-white counterpane on it, a marble-topped washstand, grayish coarse lace curtains on strings at the two small windows, a small closed fireplace with a hole in it for a stovepipe, and two trunks, standing at odds as if somebody were just moving in, or just moving out. Everything was dingy and soiled and neat and bare; not a pin out of place.

"We'll move to the St. Charles tomorrow," said Uncle Gabriel, as much to Harry as to his wife. "Get your best dresses together, Honey, the long dry spell is over."

Miss Honey's nostrils pinched together and she rocked slightly, with her arms folded. "I've lived in the St. Charles before, and I've lived here before," she said, in a tight deliberate voice, "and this time I'll just stay where I am, thank you. I prefer it to moving back here in three months. I'm settled now, I feel at home here," she told him, glancing at Harry, her pale eyes kindling with blue fire, a stiff white line around her mouth.

The little girls sat trying not to stare, miserably ill at ease. Their grandmother had pronounced Harry's children to be the most unteachable she had ever seen in her long experience with the young; but they had learned by indirection one thing well—nice people did not carry on quarrels before outsiders. Family quarrels were sacred, to be waged privately in fierce hissing whispers, low choked mutters and growls. If they did yell and stamp, it must be behind closed doors and windows. Uncle Gabriel's second wife was hopping mad and she looked ready to fly out at Uncle Gabriel any second, with him sitting there like a hound when someone shakes a whip at him.

"She loathes and despises everybody in this room," thought Miranda, coolly, "and she's afraid we won't know it. She needn't worry, we knew it when we came in." With all her heart she wanted to go, but her father, though his face was a study, made no move. He seemed to be trying to think of something pleasant to say. Maria, feeling guilty, though she couldn't think why, was calculating rapidly, "Why, she's only Uncle Gabriel's second wife, and Uncle Gabriel was only married before to Aunt Amy, why, she's no kin at all, and I'm glad of it." Sitting back easily, she let her hands fall open in her lap; they would be going in a few minutes, undoubtedly, and they need never come back.

Then father said, "We mustn't be keeping you, we just dropped in for a few minutes. We wanted to see how you are."

Miss Honey said nothing, but she made a little gesture with her hands, from the wrist, as if to say, "Well, you see how I am, and now what next?"

"I must take these young ones back to school," said father, and Uncle Gabriel said stupidly, "Look, Honey, don't you think they resemble Amy a little? Especially around the eyes, especially Maria, don't you think, Harry?"

Their father glanced at them in turn. "I really couldn't say," he decided, and the little girls saw he was more monstrously embarrassed than ever. He turned to Miss Honey, "I hadn't seen Gabriel for so many years," he said, "we thought of getting out for a talk about old times together. You know how it is."

"Yes, I know," said Miss Honey, rocking a little, and all that she knew gleamed forth in a pallid, unquenchable hatred and bitterness that seemed enough to bring her long body straight up out of the chair in a fury, "I know," and she sat staring at the floor. Her mouth shook and straightened. There was a terrible silence, which was broken when the little girls saw their father rise. They got up, too, and it was all they could do to keep from making a dash for the door.

"I must get the young ones back," said their father. "They've had enough excitement for one day. They each won a hundred dollars on Miss Lucy. It was a good race," he said, in complete wretchedness, as if he simply could not extricate himself from the situation. "Wasn't it, Gabriel?"

"It was a grand race," said Gabriel, brokenly, "a grand race."

Miss Honey stood up and moved a step towards the door. "Do you take them to the races, actually?" she asked, and her lids flickered towards them as if they were loathsome insects, Maria felt.

"If I feel they deserve a little treat, yes," said their father, in an easy tone but with wrinkled brow.

"I had rather, much rather," said Miss Honey clearly, "see my son dead at my feet than hanging around a race track."

The next few moments were rather a blank, but at last they were out of it, going down the stairs, across the patio, with Uncle Gabriel seeing them back into the cab. His face was sagging, the features had fallen as if the flesh had slipped from the bones, and his eyelids were puffed and blue. "Good-by, Harry," he said soberly. "How long you expect to be here?"

"Starting back tomorrow," said Harry. "Just dropped in on a little business and to see how the girls were getting along."

"Well," said Uncle Gabriel, "I may be dropping into your part of the country one of these days. Good-by, children," he said, taking their hands one after the other in his big warm paws. "They're nice children, Harry. I'm glad you won on Miss Lucy," he said to the little girls, tenderly. "Don't spend your money foolishly, now. Well, so long, Harry." As the cab jolted away he stood there fat and sagging, holding up his arm and wagging his hand at them.

"Goodness," said Maria, in her most grown-up manner, taking her hat off and hanging it over her knee, "I'm glad that's over."

"What I want to know is," said Miranda, "*is* Uncle Gabriel a real drunkard?"

"Oh, hush," said their father, sharply, "I've got the heartburn."

There was a respectful pause, as before a public monument. When their father had the heartburn it was time to lay low. The cab rumbled on, back to clean gay streets, with the lights coming on in the early February darkness, past shimmering shop windows, smooth pavements, on and on, past beautiful old houses set in deep gardens, on, on back to the dark walls with the heavy-topped trees hanging over them. Miranda sat thinking so hard she forgot and spoke out in her thoughtless way: "I've decided I'm not going to be a jockey, after all." She could as usual have bitten her tongue, but as usual it was too late.

Father cheered up and twinkled at her knowingly, as if that didn't surprise him in the least. "Well, well," said he, "so you aren't going to be a jockey! That's very sensible of you. I think she ought to be a lion-tamer, don't you, Maria? That's a nice, womanly profession."

Miranda, seeing Maria from the height of her fourteen years suddenly joining with their father to laugh at her, made an instant decision and laughed with them at herself. That was better. Everybody laughed and it was such a relief.

"Where's my hundred dollars?" asked Maria, anxiously.

"It's going in the bank," said their father, "and yours too," he told Miranda. "That is your nest-egg."

"Just so they don't buy my stockings with it," said Miranda, who had long resented the use of her Christmas money by their grandmother. "I've got enough stockings to last me a year."

"I'd like to buy a racehorse," said Maria, "but I know it's not enough." The limitations of wealth oppressed her. "*What* could you buy with a hundred dollars?" she asked fretfully.

"Nothing, nothing at all," said their father, "a hundred dollars is just something you put in the bank."

Maria and Miranda lost interest. They had won a hundred dollars on a horse race once. It was already in the far past. They began to chatter about something else.

The lay sister opened the door on a long cord, from behind the grille; Maria and Miranda walked in silently to their familiar world of shining bare floors and insipid wholesome food and cold-water washing and regular prayers; their world of poverty, chastity and obedience, of early to bed and early to rise, of sharp little rules and tittle-tattle. Resignation was in their childish faces as they held them up to be kissed.

"Be good girls," said their father, in the strange serious, rather helpless way he always had when he told them good-by. "Write to your daddy, now, nice long letters," he said, holding their arms firmly for a moment before letting go for good. Then he disappeared, and the sister swung the door closed after him.

Maria and Miranda went upstairs to the dormitory to wash their faces and hands and slick down their hair again before supper.

Miranda was hungry. "We didn't have a thing to eat after all," she grumbled. "Not even a chocolate nut bar. I think that's mean. We didn't even get a quarter to spend," she said.

"Not a living bite," said Maria. "Not a nickel." She poured out cold water into the bowl and rolled up her sleeves.

Another girl about her own age came in and went to a washbowl near another bed. "Where have you been?" she asked. "Did you have a good time?"

"We went to the races, with our father," said Maria, soaping her hands.

"Our uncle's horse won," said Miranda.

"My goodness," said the other girl, vaguely, "that must have been grand."

Maria looked at Miranda, who was rolling up her own sleeves. She tried to feel martyred, but it wouldn't go. "Immured for another week," she said, her eyes sparkling over the edge of her towel.

PART III: 1912

Miranda followed the porter down the stuffy aisle of the sleeping-car, where the berths were nearly all made down and the dusty green curtains buttoned, to a seat at the further end. "Now yo' berth's ready any time, Miss," said the porter.

"But I want to sit up a while," said Miranda. A very thin old lady raised choleric black eyes and fixed upon her a regard of unmixed disapproval. She had two immense front teeth and a receding chin, but she did not lack character. She had piled her luggage around her like a barricade, and she glared at the porter when he picked some of it up to make room for his new passenger. Miranda sat, saying mechanically, "May I?"

"You may, indeed," said the old lady, for she seemed old in spite of a certain brisk, rustling energy. Her taffeta petticoats creaked like hinges every time she stirred. With ferocious sarcasm, after a half second's pause, she added, "You may be so good as to get off my hat!"

Miranda rose instantly in horror, and handed to the old lady a wilted contrivance of black horsehair braid and shattered white poppies. "I'm dreadfully sorry," she stammered, for she had been brought up to treat ferocious old ladies respectfully, and this one seemed capable of spanking her, then and there. "I didn't dream it was your hat."

"And whose hat did you dream it might be?" inquired the old lady, baring her teeth and twirling the hat on a forefinger to restore it.

"I didn't think it was a hat at all," said Miranda with a touch of hysteria.

"Oh, you didn't think it was a hat? Where on earth are your eyes, child?" and she proved the nature and function of the object by placing it on her head at a somewhat tipsy angle, though still it did not much resemble a hat. "Now can you see what it is?"

"Yes, oh, yes," said Miranda, with a meekness she hoped was disarming. She ventured to sit again after a careful inspection of the narrow space she was to occupy.

"Well, well," said the old lady, "let's have the porter remove some of these encumbrances," and she stabbed the bell with a lean sharp forefinger. There followed a flurry of rearrangements, during which they both stood in the aisle, the old lady giving a series of impossible directions to the Negro which he bore philosophically while he disposed of the luggage exactly as he had meant to do. Seated again, the old lady asked in a kindly, authoritative tone, "And what might your name be, child?"

At Miranda's answer, she blinked somewhat, unfolded her spectacles, straddled them across her high nose competently, and took a good long look at the face beside her.

"If I'd had my spectacles on," she said, in an astonishingly changed voice, "I might have known. I'm Cousin Eva Parrington," she said, "Cousin Molly Parrington's daughter, remember? I knew you when you were a little girl. You were a lively little girl," she added as if to console her, "and very opinionated. The last thing I heard about you, you were planning to be a tightrope walker. You were going to play the violin and walk the tight rope at the same time."

"I must have seen it at the vaudeville show," said Miranda. "I couldn't have invented it. Now I'd like to be an air pilot!"

"I used to go to dances with your father," said Cousin Eva, busy with her own thoughts, "and to big holiday parties at your grandmother's house, long before you were born. Oh, indeed, yes, a long time before."

Miranda remembered several things at once. Aunt Amy had threatened to be an old maid like Eva. Oh, Eva, the trouble with her is she has no chin. Eva has given up, and is teaching Latin in a Female Seminary. Eva's gone out for votes for women, God help her. The nice thing about an ugly daughter is, she's not apt to make me a grandmother. . . . "They didn't do you much good, those parties, dear Cousin Eva," thought Miranda.

"They didn't do me much good, those parties," said Cousin Eva aloud as if she were a mind-reader, and Miranda's head swam for a moment with fear that she had herself spoken aloud. "Or at least, they didn't serve their purpose, for I never got married; but I enjoyed them, just the same. I had a good time at those parties, even if I wasn't a belle. And so you are Harry's child, and here I was quarreling with you. You do remember me, don't you?"

"Yes," said Miranda, and thinking that even if Cousin Eva had been really an old maid ten years before, still she couldn't be much past fifty now, and she looked so withered and tired, so famished and sunken in the cheeks, so *old*, somehow. Across the abyss separating Cousin Eva from her own youth, Miranda looked with painful premonition. "Oh, must I ever be like that?" She said aloud, "Yes, you used to read Latin to me, and tell me not to bother about the sense, to get the sound in my mind, and it would come easier later."

"Ah, so I did," said Cousin Eva, delighted. "So I did. You don't happen to remember that I once had a beautiful sapphire velvet dress with a train on it?"

"No, I don't remember that dress," said Miranda.

"It was an old dress of my mother's made over and cut down to fit," said Eva, "and it wasn't in the least becoming to me, but it was the only really good dress I ever had, and I remember it as if it were yesterday. Blue was never my color." She sighed with a humorous bitterness. The humor seemed momentary, but the bitterness was a constant state of mind.

Miranda, trying to offer the sympathy of fellow suffering, said, "I know. I've had Maria's dresses made over for me, and they were never right. It was dreadful."

"Well," said Cousin Eva, in the tone of one who did not wish to share her unique disappointments. "How is your father? I always liked him. He was one of the finest-looking young men I ever saw. Vain, too, like all his family. He wouldn't ride any but the best horses he could buy, and I used to say he made them prance and then watched his own shadow. I used to tell this on him at dinner parties, and he hated me for it. I feel pretty certain he hated me." An overtone of complacency in Cousin Eva's voice explained better than words that she had her own method of commanding attention and arousing emotion. "How *is* your father, I asked you, my dear?"

"I haven't seen him for nearly a year," answered Miranda, quickly, before Cousin Eva could get ahead again. "I'm going home now to Uncle Gabriel's funeral; you know, Uncle Gabriel died in Lexington and they have brought him back to be buried beside Aunt Amy."

"So that's how we meet," said Cousin Eva. "Yes, Gabriel drank himself to death at last. I'm going to the funeral, too. I haven't been home since I went to Mother's funeral, it must be, let's see, yes, it will be nine years next July. I'm going to Gabriel's funeral, though. I wouldn't miss that. Poor fellow, what a life he had. Pretty soon, they'll all be gone."

Miranda said, "We're left, Cousin Eva," meaning those of her own generation, the young, and Cousin Eva said, "Pshaw, you'll live forever, and you won't bother to come to our funerals." She didn't seem to think this was a misfortune, but flung the remark from her like a woman accustomed to saying what she thought.

Miranda sat thinking, "Still, I suppose it would be pleasant if I could say something to make her believe that she and all of them would be lamented, but—but—" With a smile which she hoped would be her denial of Cousin Eva's cynicism about the younger generation, she said, "You were right about the Latin, Cousin Eva, your reading did help when I began with it. I still study," she said. "Latin, too."

"And why shouldn't you?" asked Cousin Eva, sharply, adding at once mildly, "I'm glad you are going to use your mind a little, child. Don't let yourself rust away. Your mind outwears all sorts of things you may set your heart upon; you can enjoy it when all other things are taken away." Miranda was chilled by her melancholy. Cousin Eva went on: "In our part of the country, in my time, we were so provincial—a woman didn't dare to think or act for herself. The whole world was a little that way," she said, "but we were the worst, I believe. I suppose you must know how I fought for votes for women when it almost made a pariah of me—I was turned out of my chair at the Seminary, but I'm glad I did it and I would do it again. You young things don't realize. You'll live in a better world because we worked for it."

Miranda knew something of Cousin Eva's career. She said sincerely, "I think it was brave of you, and I'm glad you did it, too. I loved your courage."

"It wasn't just showing off, mind you," said Cousin Eva, rejecting praise, fretfully. "Any fool can be brave. We were working for something we knew was right, and it turned out that we needed a lot of courage for it. That was all. I didn't expect to go to jail, but I went three times, and I'd go three times three more if it were necessary. We aren't voting yet," she said, "but we will be."

Miranda did not venture any answer, but she felt convinced that indeed women would be voting soon if nothing fatal happened to Cousin Eva. There was something in her manner which said such things could be left safely to her. Miranda was dimly fired for the cause herself; it seemed heroic and worth suffering for, but discouraging, too, to those who came after: Cousin Eva so plainly had swept the field clear of opportunity.

They were silent for a few minutes, while Cousin Eva rummaged in her handbag, bringing up odds and ends: peppermint drops, eye drops, a packet of needles, three handkerchiefs, a little bottle of violet perfume, a book of addresses, two buttons, one black, one white, and, finally, a packet of headache powders.

"Bring me a glass of water, will you, my dear?" she asked Miranda. She poured the headache powder on her tongue, swallowed the water, and put two peppermints in her mouth.

"So now they're going to bury Gabriel near Amy," she said after a while, as if her eased headache had started her on a new train of thought. "Miss Honey would like that, poor dear, if she could know. After listening to stories about Amy for twenty-five years, she must lie alone in her grave in Lexington while Gabriel sneaks off to Texas to make his bed with Amy again. It was a kind of life-long infidelity, Miranda, and now an eternal infidelity on top of that. He ought to be ashamed of himself."

"It was Aunt Amy he loved," said Miranda, wondering what Miss Honey could have been like before her long troubles with Uncle Gabriel. "First, anyway."

"Oh, that Amy," said Cousin Eva, her eyes glittering. "Your Aunt Amy was a devil and a mischief-maker, but I loved her dearly. I used to stand up for Amy when her reputation wasn't worth that." Her fingers snapped like castanets. "She used to say to me, in that gay soft way she had, 'Now, Eva, don't go talking votes for women when the lads ask you to dance. Don't recite Latin poems to 'em,' she would say, 'they got sick of that in school. Dance and say nothing, Eva,' she would say, her eyes perfectly devilish, 'and hold your chin up, Eva.' My chin was my weak point, you see. 'You'll never catch a husband if you don't look out,' she would say. Then she would laugh and fly away, and where did she fly to?" demanded Cousin Eva, her sharp eyes pinning Miranda down to the bitter facts of the case, "To scandal and to death, nowhere else."

"She was joking, Cousin Eva," said Miranda, innocently, "and everybody loved her."

"Not everybody, by a long shot," said Cousin Eva in triumph. "She had enemies. If she knew, she pretended she didn't. If she cared, she never said. You couldn't make her quarrel. She was sweet as a honeycomb to everybody. *Everybody*," she added, "that was the trouble. She went through life like a spoiled darling, doing as she pleased and letting other people suffer for it, and pick up the pieces after her. I never believed for one moment," said Cousin Eva, putting her mouth close to Miranda's ear and breathing peppermint hotly into it, "that Amy was an impure woman. Never! But let me tell you, there were plenty who did believe it. There were plenty to pity poor Gabriel for being so completely blinded by her. A great many persons were not surprised when they heard that Gabriel was perfectly miserable all the time, on their honeymoon, in New Orleans. Jealousy. And why not? But I used to say to such persons that, no matter what the appearances were, I had faith in Amy's virtue. Wild, I said, indiscreet, I said, heartless, I said, but *virtuous*, I feel certain. But you could hardly blame anyone for being mystified. The way she rose up suddenly from death's door to marry Gabriel Breaux, after refusing him and treating him like a dog for years, looked odd, to say the least. To say the very least," she added, after a moment, "odd is a mild word for it. And there was something very mysterious about her death, only six weeks after marriage."

Miranda roused herself. She felt she knew this part of the story and could set Cousin Eva right about one thing. "She died of a hemorrhage from the lungs," said Miranda. "She had been ill for five years, don't you remember?"

Cousin Eva was ready for that. "Ha, that was the story, indeed. The official account, you might say. Oh, yes, I heard that often enough. But did you ever hear about that fellow Raymond somebody-or-other from Calcasieu Parish, almost a stranger, who persuaded Amy to elope with him from a dance one night, and she just ran out into the darkness without even stopping for her cloak, and your poor dear nice father Harry—you weren't even thought of then—had to run him down to earth and shoot him?"

Miranda leaned back from the advancing flood of speech. "Cousin Eva, my father shot *at* him, don't you remember? He didn't hit him. . . ."

"Well, that's a pity."

". . . and they had only gone out for a breath of air between dances. It was Uncle Gabriel's jealousy. And my father shot at the man because he thought that was better than letting Uncle Gabriel fight a duel about Aunt Amy. There was *nothing* in the whole affair except Uncle Gabriel's jealousy."

"You poor baby," said Cousin Eva, and pity gave a light like daggers to her eyes, "you dear innocent, you —do you believe that? How old are you, anyway?"

"Just past eighteen," said Miranda.

"If you don't understand what I tell you," said Cousin Eva portentously, "you will later. Knowledge can't hurt you. You mustn't live in a romantic haze about life. You'll understand when you're married, at any rate."

"I'm married now, Cousin Eva," said Miranda, feeling for almost the first time that it might be an advantage, "nearly a year. I eloped from school." It seemed very unreal even as she said it, and seemed to have nothing at all to do with the future; still, it was important, it must be declared, it was a situation in life which people seemed to be most exacting about, and the only feeling she could rouse in herself about it was an immense weariness as if it were an illness that she might one day hope to recover from.

"Shameful, shameful," cried Cousin Eva, genuinely repelled. "If you had been my child I should have brought you home and spanked you."

Miranda laughed out. Cousin Eva seemed to believe things could be arranged like that. She was so solemn and fierce, so comic and baffled.

"And you must know I should have just gone straight out again, through the nearest window," she taunted her. "If I went the first time, why not the second?"

"Yes, I suppose so," said Cousin Eva. "I hope you married rich."

"Not so very," said Miranda. "Enough." As if anyone could have stopped to think of such a thing!

Cousin Eva adjusted her spectacles and sized up Miranda's dress, her luggage, examined her engagement ring and wedding ring, with her nostrils fairly quivering as if she might smell out wealth on her.

"Well, that's better than nothing," said Cousin Eva. "I thank God every day of my life that I have a small income. It's a Rock of Ages. What would have become of me if I hadn't a cent of my own? Well, you'll be able now to do something for your family."

Miranda remembered what she had always heard about the Parringtons. They were money-hungry, they loved money and nothing else, and when they had got some they kept it. Blood was thinner than water between the Parringtons where money was concerned.

"We're pretty poor," said Miranda, stubbornly allying herself with her father's family instead of her husband's, "but a rich marriage is no way out," she said, with the snobbishness of poverty. She was thinking, "You don't know my branch of the family, dear Cousin Eva, if you think it is."

"Your branch of the family," said Cousin Eva, with that terrifying habit she had of lifting phrases out of one's mind, "has no more practical sense than so many children. Everything for love," she said, with a face of positive nausea, "that was it. Gabriel would have been rich if his grandfather had not disinherited him, but would Amy be sensible and marry him and make him settle down so the old man would have been pleased with him? No. And what could Gabriel do without money? I wish you could have seen the life he led Miss Honey, one day buying her Paris gowns and the next day pawning her earrings. It just depended on how the horses ran, and they ran worse and worse, and Gabriel drank more and more."

Miranda did not say, "I saw a little of it." She was trying to imagine Miss Honey in a Paris gown. She said, "But Uncle Gabriel was so mad about Aunt Amy, there was no question of her not marrying him at last, money or no money."

Cousin Eva strained her lips tightly over her teeth, let them fly again and leaned over, gripping Miranda's arm. "What I ask myself, what I ask myself over and over again," she whispered, "is, what connection did this man Raymond from Calcasieu have with Amy's sudden marriage to Gabriel, and *what* did Amy do to make away with herself so soon afterward? For mark my words, child, Amy wasn't so ill as all that. She'd been flying around for years after the doctors said her lungs were weak. Amy did away with herself to escape some disgrace, some exposure that she faced."

The beady black eyes glinted; Cousin Eva's face was quite frightening, so near and so intent. Miranda wanted to say, "Stop. Let her rest. What harm did she ever do you?" but she was timid and unnerved, and deep in her was a horrid fascination with the terrors and the darkness Cousin Eva had conjured up. What was the end of this story?

"She was a bad, wild girl, but I was fond of her to the last," said Cousin Eva. "She got into trouble somehow, and she couldn't get out again, and I have every reason to believe she killed herself with the drug they gave her to keep her quiet after a hemorrhage. If she didn't, what happened, what happened?"

"I don't know," said Miranda. "How should I know?

She was very beautiful," she said, as if this explained everything. "Everybody said she was very beautiful."

"Not everybody," said Cousin Eva, firmly, shaking her head. "I for one never thought so. They made entirely too much fuss over her. She was good-looking enough, but why did they think she was beautiful? I cannot understand it. She was too thin when she was young, and later I always thought she was too fat, and again in her last year she was altogether too thin. She always got herself up to be looked at, and so people looked, of course. She rode too hard, and she danced too freely, and she talked too much, and you'd have to be blind, deaf and dumb not to notice her. I don't mean she was loud or vulgar, she wasn't, but she was *too free*," said Cousin Eva. She stopped for breath and put a peppermint in her mouth. Miranda could see Cousin Eva on the platform, making her speeches, stopping to take a peppermint. But why did she hate Aunt Amy so, when Aunt Amy was dead and she alive? Wasn't being alive enough?

"And her illness wasn't romantic either," said Cousin Eva, "though to hear them tell it she faded like a lily. Well, she coughed blood, if that's romantic. If they had made her take proper care of herself, if she had been nursed sensibly, she might have been alive today. But no, nothing of the kind. She lay wrapped in beautiful shawls on a sofa with flowers around her, eating as she liked or not eating, getting up after a hemorrhage and going out to ride or dance, sleeping with the windows closed; with crowds coming in and out laughing and talking at all hours, and Amy sitting up so her hair wouldn't get out of curl. And why wouldn't that sort of thing kill a well person in time? I have almost died twice in my life," said Cousin Eva, "and both times I was sent to a hospital where I belonged and left there until I came out. And I came out," she said, her voice deepening to a bugle note, "and I went to work again."

"Beauty goes, character stays," said the small voice of axiomatic morality in Miranda's ear. It was a dreary prospect; why was a strong character so deforming? Miranda felt she truly wanted to be strong, but how could she face it, seeing what it did to one?

"She had a lovely complexion," said Cousin Eva, "perfectly transparent with a flush on each cheekbone. But it was tuberculosis, and is disease beautiful? And she brought it on herself by drinking lemon and salt to stop her periods when she wanted to go to dances. There was a superstition among young girls about that. They fancied that young men could tell what ailed them by touching their hands, or even by looking at them. As if it mattered? But they were terribly self-conscious and they had immense respect for man's worldly wisdom in those days. My own notion is that a man couldn't—but anyway, the whole thing was stupid."

"I should have thought they'd have stayed at home if they couldn't manage better than that," said Miranda, feeling very knowledgeable and modern.

"They didn't dare. Those parties and dances were their market, a girl couldn't afford to miss out, there were always rivals waiting to cut the ground from under her. The rivalry—" said Cousin Eva, and her head lifted, she arched like a cavalry horse getting a whiff of the battlefield—"you can't imagine what the rivalry was like. The way those girls treated each other—nothing was too mean, nothing too false—"

Cousin Eva wrung her hands. "It was just sex," she

said in despair; "their minds dwelt on nothing else. They didn't call it that, it was all smothered under pretty names, but that's all it was, sex." She looked out of the window into the darkness, her sunken cheek near Miranda flushed deeply. She turned back. "I took to the soap box and the platform when I was called upon," she said proudly, "and I went to jail when it was necessary, and my condition didn't make any difference. I was booed and jeered and shoved around just as if I had been in perfect health. But it was part of our philosophy not to let our physical handicaps make any difference to our work. You know what I mean," she said, as if until now it was all mystery. "Well, Amy carried herself with more spirit than the others, and she didn't seem to be making any sort of fight, but she was simply sex-ridden, like the rest. She behaved as if she hadn't a rival on earth, and she pretended not to know what marriage was about, but I know better. None of them had, and they didn't want to have, anything else to think about, and they didn't really know anything about that, so they simply festered inside—they festered—"

Miranda found herself deliberately watching a long procession of living corpses, festering women stepping gaily towards the charnel house, their corruption concealed under laces and flowers, their dead faces lifted smiling, and thought quite coldly, "Of course it was not like that. This is no more true than what I was told before, it's every bit as romantic," and she realized that she was tired of her intense Cousin Eva, she wanted to go to sleep, she wanted to be at home, she wished it were tomorrow and she could see her father and her sister, who were so alive and solid; who would mention her freckles and ask her if she wanted something to eat.

"My mother was not like that," she said, childishly. "My mother was a perfectly natural woman who liked to cook. I have seen some of her sewing," she said. "I have read her diary."

"Your mother was a saint," said Cousin Eva, automatically.

Miranda sat silent, outraged. "My mother was nothing of the sort," she wanted to fling in Cousin Eva's big front teeth. But Cousin Eva had been gathering bitterness until more speech came of it.

" 'Hold your chin up, Eva,' Amy used to tell me," she began, doubling up both her fists and shaking them a little. "All my life the whole family bedeviled me about my chin. My entire girlhood was spoiled by it. Can you imagine," she asked, with a ferocity that seemed much too deep for this one cause, "people who call themselves civilized spoiling life for a young girl because she had one unlucky feature? Of course, you understand perfectly it was all in the very best humor, everybody was very amusing about it, no harm meant—oh, no, no harm at all. That is the hellish thing about it. It is that I can't forgive," she cried out, and she twisted her hands together as if they were rags. "Ah, the family," she said, releasing her breath and sitting back quietly, "the whole hideous institution should be wiped from the face of the earth. It is the root of all human wrongs," she ended, and relaxed, and her face became calm. She was trembling. Miranda reached out and took Cousin Eva's hand and held it. The hand fluttered and lay still, and Cousin Eva said, "You've not the faintest idea what some of us went through, but I wanted you to hear the other side of the story. And I'm keeping you up when you need your beauty sleep," she said grimly, stirring herself with an immense rustle of petticoats.

Miranda pulled herself together, feeling limp, and stood up. Cousin Eva put out her hand again, and drew Miranda down to her. "Good night, you dear child," she said, "to think you're grown up." Miranda hesitated, then quite suddenly kissed her Cousin Eva on the cheek. The black eyes shone brightly through water for an instant, and Cousin Eva said with a warm note in her sharp clear orator's voice, "Tomorrow we'll be at home again. I'm looking forward to it, aren't you? Good night."

Miranda fell asleep while she was getting off her clothes. Instantly it was morning again. She was still trying to close her suitcase when the train pulled into the small station, and there on the platform she saw her father, looking tired and anxious, his hat pulled over his eyes. She rapped on the window to catch his attention, then ran out and threw herself upon him. He said, "Well, here's my big girl," as if she were still seven, but his hands on her arms held her off, the tone was forced. There was no welcome for her, and there had not been since she had run away. She could not persuade herself to remember how it would be; between one home-coming and the next her mind refused to accept its own knowledge. Her father looked over her head and said, without surprise, "Why, hello, Eva, I'm glad somebody sent you a telegram." Miranda, rebuffed again, let her arms fall away again, with the same painful dull jerk of the heart.

"No one in my family," said Eva, her face framed in the thin black veil she reserved, evidently, for family funerals, "ever sent me a telegram in my life. I had the

65

news from young Keziah who had it from young Gabriel. I suppose Gabe is here?"

"Everybody seems to be here," said Father. "The
house is getting full."

"I'll go to the hotel if you like," said Cousin Eva.

"Damnation, no," said Father. "I didn't mean that.
You'll come with us where you belong."

Skid, the handy man, grabbed the suitcases and started
down the rocky village street. "We've got the car," said
Father. He took Miranda by the hand, then dropped it
again, and reached for Cousin Eva's elbow.

"I'm perfectly able, thank you," said Cousin Eva,
shying away.

"If you're so independent now," said Father, "God
help us when you get that vote."

Cousin Eva pushed back her veil. She was smiling
merrily. She liked Harry, she always had liked him, he
could tease as much as he liked. She slipped her arm
through his. "So it's all over with poor Gabriel, isn't
it?"

"Oh, yes," said Father, "it's all over, all right. They're
pegging out pretty regularly now. It will be our turn
next, Eva?"

"I don't know, and I don't care," said Eva, recklessly.
"It's good to be back now and then, Harry, even if it is
only for funerals. I feel sinfully cheerful."

"Oh, Gabriel wouldn't mind, he'd like seeing you
cheerful. Gabriel was the cheerfulest cuss I ever saw,
when we were young. Life for Gabriel," said Father,
"was just one perpetual picnic."

"Poor fellow," said Cousin Eva.

"Poor old Gabriel," said Father, heavily.

Miranda walked along beside her father, feeling home-

66

less, but not sorry for it. He had not forgiven her, she knew that. When would he? She could not guess, but she felt it would come of itself, without words and without acknowledgment on either side, for by the time it arrived neither of them would need to remember what had caused their division, nor why it had seemed so important. Surely old people cannot hold their grudges forever because the young want to live, too, she thought, in her arrogance, her pride. I will make my own mistakes, not yours; I cannot depend upon you beyond a certain point, why depend at all? There was something more beyond, but this was a first step to take, and she took it, walking in silence beside her elders who were no longer Cousin Eva and Father, since they had forgotten her presence, but had become Eva and Harry, who knew each other well, who were comfortable with each other, being contemporaries on equal terms, who occupied by right their place in this world, at the time of life to which they had arrived by paths familiar to them both. They need not play their roles of daughter, of son, to aged persons who did not understand them; nor of father and elderly female cousin to young persons whom they did not understand. They were precisely themselves; their eyes cleared, their voices relaxed into perfect naturalness, they need not weigh their words or calculate the effect of their manner. "It is I who have no place," thought Miranda. "Where are my own people and my own time?" She resented, slowly and deeply and in profound silence, the presence of these aliens who lectured and admonished her, who loved her with bitterness and denied her the right to look at the world with her own eyes, who demanded that she accept their version of life and yet could not tell her the truth, not in the smallest thing. "I hate them both," her most inner and secret mind said plainly, "*I will be free of them, I shall not even remember them.*"

She sat in the front seat with Skid, the Negro boy. "Come back with us, Miranda," said Cousin Eva, with the sharp little note of elderly command, "there is plenty of room."

"No, thank you," said Miranda, in a firm cold voice. "I'm quite comfortable. Don't disturb yourself."

Neither of them noticed her voice or her manner. They sat back and went on talking steadily in their friendly family voices, talking about their dead, their living, their affairs, their prospects, their common memories, interrupting each other, catching each other up on small points of dispute, laughing with a gaiety and freshness Miranda had not known they were capable of, going over old stories and finding new points of interest in them.

Miranda could not hear the stories above the noisy motor, but she felt she knew them well, or stories like them. She knew too many stories like them, she wanted something new of her own. The language was familiar to them, but not to her, not any more. The house, her father had said, was full. It would be full of cousins, many of them strangers. Would there be any young cousins there, to whom she could talk about things they both knew? She felt a vague distaste for seeing cousins. There were too many of them and her blood rebelled against the ties of blood. She was sick to death of cousins. She did not want any more ties with this house, she was going to leave it, and she was not going back to her husband's family either. She would have no more bonds that smothered her in love and hatred. She knew now why she had run away to marriage, and she knew that she was going to run away from marriage, and she was not going to stay in any place, with anyone, that threatened to forbid her making her own discoveries, that said "No" to her. She hoped no one had taken her old room, she would like to sleep there once more, she would say good-by there where she had loved sleeping once, sleeping and waking and waiting to be grown, to begin to live. Oh, what is life, she asked herself in desperate seriousness, in those childish unanswerable words, and what shall I do with it? It is something of my own, she thought in a fury of jealous possessiveness, what shall I make of it? She did not know that she asked herself this because all her earliest training had argued that life was a substance, a material to be used, it took shape and direction and meaning only as the possessor guided and worked it; living was a progress of continuous and varied acts of the will directed towards a definite end. She had been assured that there were good and evil ends, one must make a choice. But what was good, and what was evil? I hate love, she thought, as if this were the answer, I hate loving and being loved, I hate it. And her disturbed and seething mind received a shock of comfort from this sudden collapse of an old painful structure of distorted images and misconceptions. "You don't know anything about it," said Miranda to herself, with extraordinary clearness as if she were an elder admonishing some younger misguided creature. "You have to find out about it." But nothing in her prompted her to decide, "I will now do this, I will be that, I will go yonder, I will take a certain road to a certain end." There are questions to be asked first, she thought, but who will answer them? No one, or there will be too many answers none of them right. What is the truth, she asked herself as intently as if the question had never been asked, the truth, even about the smallest, the least important of all the things I must find out? and where shall I begin to look for it? Her mind closed stubbornly against remembering, not the past but the legend of the past, other people's memory of the past, at which she had spent her life peering in wonder like a child at a magic-lantern show. Ah, but there is my own life to come yet, she thought, my own life now and beyond. I don't want any promises, I won't have false hopes, I won't be romantic about myself. I can't live in their world any longer, she told herself, listening to the voices back of her. Let them tell their stories to each other. Let them go on explaining how things happened. I don't care. At least I can know the truth about what happens to me, she assured herself silently, making a promise to herself, in her hopefulness, her ignorance.

Noon Wine

The two grubby small boys with tow-colored hair who were digging among the ragweed in the front yard sat back on their heels and said, "Hello," when the tall bony man with straw-colored hair turned in at their gate. He did not pause at the gate; it had swung back, conveniently half open, long ago, and was now sunk so firmly on its broken hinges no one thought of trying to close it. He did not even glance at the small boys, much less give them good-day. He just clumped down his big square dusty shoes one after the other steadily, like a man following a plow, as if he knew the place well and knew where he was going and what he would find there. Rounding the right-hand corner of the house under the row of chinaberry trees, he walked up to the side porch where Mr. Thompson was pushing a big swing churn back and forth.

Mr. Thompson was a tough weather-beaten man with stiff black hair and a week's growth of black whiskers. He was a noisy proud man who held his neck so straight his whole face stood level with his Adam's apple, and the whiskers continued down his neck and disappeared into a black thatch under his open collar. The churn rumbled and swished like the belly of a trotting horse, and Mr. Thompson seemed somehow to be driving a horse with one hand, reining it in and urging it forward; and every now and then he turned halfway around and squirted a tremendous spit of tobacco juice out over the steps. The door stones were brown and gleaming with fresh tobacco juice. Mr. Thompson had been churning quite a while and he was tired of it. He was just fetching a mouthful of juice to squirt again when the stranger came around the corner and stopped. Mr. Thompson saw a narrow-chested man with blue eyes so pale they were almost white, looking and not looking at him from a long gaunt face, under white eyebrows. Mr. Thompson judged him to be another of these Irishmen, by his long upper lip.

"Howdy do, sir," said Mr. Thompson politely, swinging his churn.

"I need work," said the man, clearly enough but with some kind of foreign accent Mr. Thompson couldn't place. It wasn't Cajun and it wasn't Nigger and it wasn't Dutch, so it had him stumped. "You need a man here?"

Mr. Thompson gave the churn a great shove and it swung back and forth several times on its own momentum. He sat on the steps, shot his quid into the grass, and said, "Set down. Maybe we can make a deal. I been kinda lookin' round for somebody. I had two niggers but they got into a cutting scrape up the creek last week, one of 'em dead now and the other in the hoosegow at Cold Springs. Neither one of 'em worth killing, come right down to it. So it looks like I'd better get somebody. Where'd you work last?"

"North Dakota," said the man, folding himself down on the other end of the steps, but not as if he were tired. He folded up and settled down as if it would be a long time before he got up again. He never had looked at Mr. Thompson, but there wasn't anything sneaking in his eye, either. He didn't seem to be looking anywhere else. His eyes sat in his head and let things pass by them. They didn't seem to be expecting to see anything worth looking at. Mr. Thompson waited a long time for the man to say something more, but he had gone into a brown study.

"North Dakota," said Mr. Thompson, trying to remember where that was. "That's a right smart distance off, seems to me."

"I can do everything on farm," said the man; "cheap. I need work."

Mr. Thompson settled himself to get down to business. "My name's Thompson, Mr. Royal Earle Thompson," he said.

"I'm Mr. Helton," said the man, "Mr. Olaf Helton." He did not move.

"Well, now," said Mr. Thompson in his most carrying voice, "I guess we'd better talk turkey."

When Mr. Thompson expected to drive a bargain he always grew very hearty and jovial. There was nothing wrong with him except that he hated like the devil to pay wages. He said so himself. "You furnish grub and a shack," he said, "and then you got to pay 'em besides. It ain't right. Besides the wear and tear on your implements," he said, "they just let everything go to rack and ruin." So he began to laugh and shout his way through the deal.

"Now, what I want to know is, how much you fixing to gouge outa me?" he brayed, slapping his knee. After he had kept it up as long as he could, he quieted down, feeling a little sheepish, and cut himself a chew. Mr. Helton was staring out somewhere between the barn and the orchard, and seemed to be sleeping with his eyes open.

"I'm good worker," said Mr. Helton as from the tomb. "I get dollar a day."

Mr. Thompson was so shocked he forgot to start laughing again at the top of his voice until it was nearly too late to do any good. "Haw, haw," he bawled. "Why, for a dollar a day I'd hire out myself. What kinda work is it where they pay you a dollar a day?"

"Wheatfields, North Dakota," said Mr. Helton, not even smiling.

Mr. Thompson stopped laughing. "Well, this ain't any wheatfield by a long shot. This is more of a dairy farm," he said, feeling apologetic. "My wife, she was set on a dairy, she seemed to like working around with cows and calves, so I humored her. But it was a mistake," he said. "I got nearly everything to do, anyhow. My wife ain't very strong. She's sick today, that's a fact. She's been poorly for the last few days. We plant a little feed, and a corn patch, and there's the orchard, and a few pigs and chickens, but our main hold is the cows. Now just speakin' as one man to another, there ain't any money in it. Now I can't give you no dollar a day because ackshally I don't make that much out of it. No, sir, we get along on a lot less than a dollar a day, I'd say, if we figger up everything in the long run. Now, I paid seven dollars a month to the two niggers, three-fifty each, and grub, but what I say is, one middlin'-good white man ekals a whole passel of niggers any day in the week, so I'll give you seven dollars and you eat at the table with us, and you'll be treated like a white man, as the feller says—"

"That's all right," said Mr. Helton. "I take it."

"Well, now I guess we'll call it a deal, hey?" Mr. Thompson jumped up as if he had remembered important business. "Now, you just take hold of that churn and give it a few swings, will you, while I ride to town on a coupla little errands. I ain't been able to leave the place all week. I guess you know what to do with butter after you get it, don't you?"

"I know," said Mr. Helton without turning his head. "I know butter business." He had a strange drawling voice, and even when he spoke only two words his voice waved slowly up and down and the emphasis was in the wrong place. Mr. Thompson wondered what kind of foreigner Mr. Helton could be.

"Now just where did you say you worked last?" he asked, as if he expected Mr. Helton to contradict himself.

"North Dakota," said Mr. Helton.

"Well, one place is good as another once you get used to it," said Mr. Thompson, amply. "You're a forriner, ain't you?"

"I'm a Swede," said Mr. Helton, beginning to swing the churn.

Mr. Thompson let forth a booming laugh, as if this was the best joke on somebody he'd ever heard. "Well,

I'll be damned," he said at the top of his voice. "A Swede: well, now, I'm afraid you'll get pretty lonesome around here. I never seen any Swedes in this neck of the woods."

"That's all right," said Mr. Helton. He went on swinging the churn as if he had been working on the place for years.

"In fact, I might as well tell you, you're practically the first Swede I ever laid eyes on."

"That's all right," said Mr. Helton.

Mr. Thompson went into the front room where Mrs. Thompson was lying down, with the green shades drawn. She had a bowl of water by her on the table and a wet cloth over her eyes. She took the cloth off at the sound of Mr. Thompson's boots and said, "What's all the noise out there? Who is it?"

"Got a feller out there says he's a Swede, Ellie," said Mr. Thompson; "says he knows how to make butter."

"I hope it turns out to be the truth," said Mrs. Thompson. "Looks like my head never will get any better."

"Don't you worry," said Mr. Thompson. "You fret too much. Now I'm gointa ride into town and get a little order of groceries."

"Don't you linger, now, Mr. Thompson," said Mrs. Thompson. "Don't go to the hotel." She meant the saloon; the proprietor also had rooms for rent upstairs.

"Just a coupla little toddies," said Mr. Thompson, laughing loudly, "never hurt anybody."

"I never took a dram in my life," said Mrs. Thompson, "and what's more I never will."

"I wasn't talking about the womenfolks," said Mr. Thompson.

The sound of the swinging churn rocked Mrs. Thompson first into a gentle doze, then a deep drowse from which she waked suddenly knowing that the swinging had stopped a good while ago. She sat up shading her weak eyes from the flat strips of late summer sunlight between the sill and the lowered shades. There she was, thank God, still alive, with supper to cook but no churning on hand, and her head still bewildered, but easy. Slowly she realized she had been hearing a new sound even in her sleep. Somebody was playing a tune on the harmonica, not merely shrilling up and down making a sickening noise, but really playing a pretty tune, merry and sad.

She went out through the kitchen, stepped off the porch, and stood facing the east, shading her eyes. When her vision cleared and settled, she saw a long, pale-haired man in blue jeans sitting in the doorway of the hired man's shack, tilted back in a kitchen chair, blowing away at the harmonica with his eyes shut. Mrs. Thompson's heart fluttered and sank. Heavens, he looked lazy and worthless, he did, now. First a lot of no-count fiddling darkies and then a no-count white man. It was just like Mr. Thompson to take on that kind. She did wish he would be more considerate, and take a little trouble with his business. She wanted to believe in her husband, and there were too many times when she couldn't. She wanted to believe that tomorrow, or at least the day after, life, such a battle at best, was going to be better.

She walked past the shack without glancing aside, stepping carefully, bent at the waist because of the nagging pain in her side, and went to the springhouse, trying to harden her mind to speak very plainly to that new hired man if he had not done his work.

The milk house was only another shack of weather-

beaten boards nailed together hastily years before because they needed a milk house; it was meant to be
temporary, and it was; already shapeless, leaning this
way and that over a perpetual cool trickle of water that
fell from a little grot, almost choked with pallid ferns.
No one else in the whole countryside had such a spring
on his land. Mr. and Mrs. Thompson felt they had a
fortune in that spring, if ever they got around to doing
anything with it.

Rickety wooden shelves clung at hazard in the square
around the small pool where the larger pails of milk and
butter stood, fresh and sweet in the cold water. One
hand supporting her flat, pained side, the other shading
her eyes, Mrs. Thompson leaned over and peered into
the pails. The cream had been skimmed and set aside,
there was a rich roll of butter, the wooden molds and
shallow pans had been scrubbed and scalded for the first
time in who knows when, the barrel was full of butter-
milk ready for the pigs and the weanling calves, the hard
packed-dirt floor had been swept smooth. Mrs. Thompson straightened up again, smiling tenderly. She had been
ready to scold him, a poor man who needed a job, who
had just come there and who might not have been expected to do things properly at first. There was nothing
she could do to make up for the injustice she had done
him in her thoughts but to tell him how she appreciated
his good clean work, finished already, in no time at all.
She ventured near the door of the shack with her careful
steps; Mr. Helton opened his eyes, stopped playing, and
brought his chair down straight, but did not look at her,
or get up. She was a little frail woman with long thick
brown hair in a braid, a suffering patient mouth and
diseased eyes which cried easily. She wove her fingers

into an eyeshade, thumbs on temples, and, winking her tearful lids, said with a polite little manner, "Howdy do, sir. I'm Miz Thompson, and I wanted to tell you I think you did real well in the milk house. It's always been a hard place to keep."

He said, "That's all right," in a slow voice, without moving.

Mrs. Thompson waited a moment. "That's a pretty tune you're playing. Most folks don't seem to get much music out of a harmonica."

Mr. Helton sat humped over, long legs sprawling, his spine in a bow, running his thumb over the square mouth-stops; except for his moving hand he might have been asleep. The harmonica was a big shiny new one, and Mrs. Thompson, her gaze wandering about, counted five others, all good and expensive, standing in a row on the shelf beside his cot. "He must carry them around in his jumper pocket," she thought, and noted there was not a sign of any other possession lying about. "I see you're mighty fond of music," she said. "We used to have an old accordion, and Mr. Thompson could play it right smart, but the little boys broke it up."

Mr. Helton stood up rather suddenly, the chair clattered under him, his knees straightened though his shoulders did not, and he looked at the floor as if he were listening carefully. "You know how little boys are," said Mrs. Thompson. "You'd better set them harmonicas on a high shelf or they'll be after them. They're great hands for getting into things. I try to learn 'em, but it don't do much good."

Mr. Helton, in one wide gesture of his long arms, swept his harmonicas up against his chest, and from there transferred them in a row to the ledge where the roof joined to the wall. He pushed them back almost out of sight.

"That'll do, maybe," said Mrs. Thompson. "Now I wonder," she said, turning and closing her eyes helplessly against the stronger western light, "I wonder what became of them little tads. I can't keep up with them." She had a way of speaking about her children as if they were rather troublesome nephews on a prolonged visit.

"Down by the creek," said Mr. Helton, in his hollow voice. Mrs. Thompson, pausing confusedly, decided he had answered her question. He stood in silent patience, not exactly waiting for her to go, perhaps, but pretty plainly not waiting for anything else. Mrs. Thompson was perfectly accustomed to all kinds of men full of all kinds of cranky ways. The point was, to find out just how Mr. Helton's crankiness was different from any other man's, and then get used to it, and let him feel at home. Her father had been cranky, her brothers and uncles had all been set in their ways and none of them alike; and every hired man she'd ever seen had quirks and crotchets of his own. Now here was Mr. Helton, who was a Swede, who wouldn't talk, and who played the harmonica besides.

"They'll be needing something to eat," said Mrs. Thompson in a vague friendly way, "pretty soon. Now I wonder what I ought to be thinking about for supper? Now what do you like to eat, Mr. Helton? We always have plenty of good butter and milk and cream, that's a blessing. Mr. Thompson says we ought to sell all of it, but I say my family comes first." Her little face went all out of shape in a pained blind smile.

"I eat anything," said Mr. Helton, his words wandering up and down.

He *can't* talk, for one thing, thought Mrs. Thompson; it's a shame to keep at him when he don't know the language good. She took a slow step away from the shack, looking back over her shoulder. "We usually have cornbread except on Sundays," she told him. "I suppose in your part of the country you don't get much good cornbread."

Not a word from Mr. Helton. She saw from her eye-corner that he had sat down again, looking at his harmonica, chair tilted. She hoped he would remember it was getting near milking time. As she moved away, he started playing again, the same tune. Milking time came and went. Mrs. Thompson saw Mr. Helton going back and forth between the cow barn and the milk house. He swung along in an easy lope, shoulders bent, head hanging, the big buckets balancing like a pair of scales at the ends of his bony arms. Mr. Thompson rode in from town sitting straighter than usual, chin in, a towsack full of supplies swung behind the saddle. After a trip to the barn, he came into the kitchen full of good will, and gave Mrs. Thompson a hearty smack on the cheek after dusting her face off with his tough whiskers. He had been to the hotel, that was plain. "Took a look around the premises, Ellie," he shouted. "That Swede sure is grinding out the labor. But he is the closest mouthed feller I ever met up with in all my days. Looks like he's scared he'll crack his jaw if he opens his front teeth."

Mrs. Thompson was stirring up a big bowl of butter-milk cornbread. "You smell like a toper, Mr. Thompson," she said with perfect dignity. "I wish you'd get one of the little boys to bring me in an extra load of firewood. I'm thinking about baking a batch of cookies tomorrow."

Mr. Thompson, all at once smelling the liquor on his own breath, sneaked out, justly rebuked, and brought in the firewood himself. Arthur and Herbert, grubby from thatched head to toes, from skin to shirt, came stamping in yelling for supper. "Go wash your faces and comb your hair," said Mrs. Thompson, automatically. They retired to the porch. Each one put his hand under the pump and wet his forelock, combed it down with his fingers, and returned at once to the kitchen, where all the fair prospects of life were centered. Mrs. Thompson set an extra plate and commanded Arthur, the eldest, eight years old, to call Mr. Helton for supper.

Arthur, without moving from the spot, bawled like a bull calf, "Saaaaaay, Helllllton, suuuuuupper's ready!" and added in a lower voice, "You big Swede!"

"Listen to me," said Mrs. Thompson, "that's no way to act. Now you go out there and ask him decent, or I'll get your daddy to give you a good licking."

Mr. Helton loomed, long and gloomy, in the doorway. "Sit right there," boomed Mr. Thompson, waving his arm. Mr. Helton swung his square shoes across the kitchen in two steps, slumped onto the bench and sat. Mr. Thompson occupied his chair at the head of the table, the two boys scrambled into place opposite Mr. Helton, and Mrs. Thompson sat at the end nearest the stove. Mrs. Thompson clasped her hands, bowed her head and said aloud hastily, "Lord, for all these and Thy other blessings we thank Thee in Jesus' name, amen," trying to finish before Herbert's rusty little paw reached the nearest dish. Otherwise she would be duty-bound to send him away from the table, and growing children need their meals. Mr. Thompson and Arthur always waited, but Herbert, aged six, was too young to take training yet.

Mr. and Mrs. Thompson tried to engage Mr. Helton in conversation, but it was a failure. They tried first the weather, and then the crops, and then the cows, but Mr. Helton simply did not reply. Mr. Thompson then told something funny he had seen in town. It was about some of the other old grangers at the hotel, friends of his, giving beer to a goat, and the goat's subsequent behavior. Mr. Helton did not seem to hear. Mrs. Thompson laughed dutifully, but she didn't think it was very funny. She had heard it often before, though Mr. Thompson, each time he told it, pretended it had happened that self-same day. It must have happened years ago if it ever happened at all, and it had never been a story that Mrs. Thompson thought suitable for mixed company. The whole thing came of Mr. Thompson's weakness for a dram too much now and then, though he voted for local option at every election. She passed the food to Mr. Helton, who took a helping of everything, but not much, not enough to keep him up to his full powers if he expected to go on working the way he had started.

At last, he took a fair-sized piece of cornbread, wiped his plate up as clean as if it had been licked by a hound dog, stuffed his mouth full, and, still chewing, slid off the bench and started for the door.

"Good night, Mr. Helton," said Mrs. Thompson, and the other Thompsons took it up in a scattered chorus. "Good night, Mr. Helton!"

"Good night," said Mr. Helton's wavering voice grudgingly from the darkness.

"Gude not," said Arthur, imitating Mr. Helton.

"Gude not," said Herbert, the copy-cat.

"You don't do it right," said Arthur. "Now listen to me. Guuuuuude naht," and he ran a hollow scale in a luxury of successful impersonation. Herbert almost went into a fit with joy.

"Now you *stop* that," said Mrs. Thompson. "He can't help the way he talks. You ought to be ashamed of yourselves, both of you, making fun of a poor stranger like that. How'd you like to be a stranger in a strange land?"

"I'd like it," said Arthur. "I think it would be fun."

"They're both regular heathens, Ellie," said Mr. Thompson. "Just plain ignoramuses." He turned the face of awful fatherhood upon his young. "You're both going to get sent to school next year, and that'll knock some sense into you."

"I'm going to git sent to the 'formatory when I'm old enough," piped up Herbert. "That's where I'm goin'."

"Oh, you are, are you?" asked Mr. Thompson. "Who says so?"

"The Sunday School Supintendant," said Herbert, a bright boy showing off.

"You see?" said Mr. Thompson, staring at his wife. "What did I tell you?" He became a hurricane of wrath. "Get to bed, you two," he roared until his Adam's apple shuddered. "Get now before I take the hide off you!" They got, and shortly from their attic bedroom the sounds of scuffling and snorting and giggling and growling filled the house and shook the kitchen ceiling.

Mrs. Thompson held her head and said in a small uncertain voice, "It's no use picking on them when they're so young and tender. I can't stand it."

"My goodness, Ellie," said Mr. Thompson, "we've got to raise 'em. We can't just let 'em grow up hog wild."

She went on in another tone. "That Mr. Helton seems all right, even if he can't be made to talk. Wonder how he comes to be so far from home."

"Like I said, he isn't no whamper-jaw," said Mr. Thompson, "but he sure knows how to lay out the work. I guess that's the main thing around here. Country's full of fellers trampin' round looking for work."

Mrs. Thompson was gathering up the dishes. She now gathered up Mr. Thompson's plate from under his chin. "To tell you the honest truth," she remarked, "I think it's a mighty good change to have a man round the place who knows how to work and keep his mouth shut. Means he'll keep out of our business. Not that we've got anything to hide, but it's convenient."

"That's a fact," said Mr. Thompson. "Haw, haw," he shouted suddenly. "Means you can do all the talking, huh?"

"The only thing," went on Mrs. Thompson, "is this: he don't eat hearty enough to suit me. I like to see a man set down and relish a good meal. My granma used to say it was no use putting dependence on a man who won't set down and make out his dinner. I hope it won't be that way this time."

"Tell *you* the truth, Ellie," said Mr. Thompson, picking his teeth with a fork and leaning back in the best of good humors, "I always thought your granma was a ter'ble ole fool. She'd just say the first thing that popped into her head and call it God's wisdom."

"My granma wasn't anybody's fool. Nine times out of ten she knew what she was talking about. I always

say, the first thing you think is the best thing you can
say."

"Well," said Mr. Thompson, going into another
shout, "you're so reefined about that goat story, you
just try speaking out in mixed comp'ny sometime! You
just try it. S'pose you happened to be thinking about a
hen and a rooster, hey? I reckon you'd shock the Babtist
preacher!" He gave her a good pinch on her thin little
rump. "No more meat on you than a rabbit," he said,
fondly. "Now I like 'em cornfed."

Mrs. Thompson looked at him open-eyed and
blushed. She could see better by lamplight. "Why, Mr.
Thompson, sometimes I think you're the evilest-minded
man that ever lived." She took a handful of hair on the
crown of his head and gave it a good, slow pull. "That's
to show you how it feels, pinching so hard when you're
supposed to be playing," she said, gently.

In spite of his situation in life, Mr. Thompson had never
been able to outgrow his deep conviction that running
a dairy and chasing after chickens was woman's work.
He was fond of saying that he could plow a furrow, cut
sorghum, shuck corn, handle a team, build a corn crib,
as well as any man. Buying and selling, too, were man's
work. Twice a week he drove the spring wagon to market
with the fresh butter, a few eggs, fruits in their proper
season, sold them, pocketed the change, and spent it as
seemed best, being careful not to dig into Mrs. Thompson's pin money.

But from the first the cows worried him, coming up
regularly twice a day to be milked, standing there re-
proaching him with their smug female faces. Calves worried him, fighting the rope and strangling themselves

until their eyes bulged, trying to get at the teat. Wrestling with a calf unmanned him, like having to change a baby's diaper. Milk worried him, coming bitter sometimes, drying up, turning sour. Hens worried him, cackling, clucking, hatching out when you least expected it and leading their broods into the barnyard where the horses could step on them; dying of roup and wryneck and getting plagues of chicken lice; laying eggs all over God's creation so that half of them were spoiled before a man could find them, in spite of a rack of nests Mrs. Thompson had set out for them in the feed room. Hens were a blasted nuisance.

Slopping hogs was hired man's work, in Mr. Thompson's opinion. Killing hogs was a job for the boss, but scraping them and cutting them up was for the hired man again; and again woman's proper work was dressing meat, smoking, pickling, and making lard and sausage. All his carefully limited fields of activity were related somehow to Mr. Thompson's feeling for the appearance of things, his own appearance in the sight of God and man. "It don't *look* right," was his final reason for not doing anything he did not wish to do.

It was his dignity and his reputation that he cared about, and there were only a few kinds of work manly enough for Mr. Thompson to undertake with his own hands. Mrs. Thompson, to whom so many forms of work would have been becoming, had simply gone down on him early. He saw, after a while, how short-sighted it had been of him to expect much from Mrs. Thompson; he had fallen in love with her delicate waist and lace-trimmed petticoats and big blue eyes, and, though all those charms had disappeared, she had in the meantime become Ellie to him, not at all the same person as Miss

Ellen Bridges, popular Sunday School teacher in the Mountain City First Baptist Church, but his dear wife, Ellie, who was not strong. Deprived as he was, however, of the main support in life which a man might expect in marriage, he had almost without knowing it resigned himself to failure. Head erect, a prompt payer of taxes, yearly subscriber to the preacher's salary, land owner and father of a family, employer, a hearty good fellow among men, Mr. Thompson knew, without putting it into words that he had been going steadily down hill. God amighty, it did look like somebody around the place might take a rake in hand now and then and clear up the clutter around the barn and the kitchen steps. The wagon shed was so full of broken-down machinery and ragged harness and old wagon wheels and battered milk pails and rotting lumber you could hardly drive in there any more. Not a soul on the place would raise a hand to it, and as for him, he had all he could do with his regular work. He would sometimes in the slack season sit for hours worrying about it, squirting tobacco on the rag-weeds growing in a thicket against the wood pile, wondering what a fellow could do, handicapped as he was. He looked forward to the boys growing up soon; he was going to put them through the mill just as his own father had done with him when he was a boy; they were going to learn how to take hold and run the place right. He wasn't going to overdo it, but those two boys were going to earn their salt, or he'd know why. Great big lubbers sitting around whittling! Mr. Thompson some-times grew quite enraged with them, when imagining their possible future, big lubbers sitting around whittling or thinking about fishing trips. Well, he'd put a stop to that, mighty damn quick.

As the seasons passed, and Mr. Helton took hold more and more, Mr. Thompson began to relax in his mind a little. There seemed to be nothing the fellow couldn't do, all in the day's work and as a matter of course. He got up at five o'clock in the morning, boiled his own coffee and fried his own bacon and was out in the cow lot before Mr. Thompson had even begun to yawn, stretch, groan, roar and thump around looking for his jeans. He milked the cows, kept the milk house, and churned the butter; rounded the hens up and somehow persuaded them to lay in the nests, not under the house and behind the haystacks; he fed them regularly and they hatched out until you couldn't set a foot down for them. Little by little the piles of trash around the barns and house disappeared. He carried buttermilk and corn to the hogs, and curried cockleburs out of the horses' manes. He was gentle with the calves, if a little grim with the cows and hens; judging by his conduct, Mr. Helton had never heard of the difference between man's and woman's work on a farm.

In the second year, he showed Mr. Thompson the picture of a cheese press in a mail order catalogue, and said, "This is a good thing. You buy this, I make cheese." The press was bought and Mr. Helton did make cheese, and it was sold, along with the increased butter and the crates of eggs. Sometimes Mr. Thompson felt a little contemptuous of Mr. Helton's ways. It did seem kind of picayune for a man to go around picking up half a dozen ears of corn that had fallen off the wagon on the way from the field, gathering up fallen fruit to feed to the pigs, storing up old nails and stray parts of machinery, spending good time stamping a fancy pattern on the butter before it went to market. Mr. Thompson, sitting up high on the spring-wagon seat, with the decorated butter in a five-gallon lard can wrapped in wet towsack, driving to town, chirruping to the horses and snapping the reins over their backs, sometimes thought that Mr. Helton was a pretty meeching sort of fellow; but he never gave way to these feelings, he knew a good thing when he had it. It was a fact the hogs were in better shape and sold for more money. It was a fact that Mr. Thompson stopped buying feed, Mr. Helton managed the crops so well. When beef- and hog-slaughtering time came, Mr. Helton knew how to save the scraps that Mr. Thompson had thrown away, and wasn't above scraping guts and filling them with sausages that he made by his own methods. In all, Mr. Thompson had no grounds for complaint. In the third year, he raised Mr. Helton's wages, though Mr. Helton had not asked for a raise. The fourth year, when Mr. Thompson was not only out of debt but had a little cash in the bank, he raised Mr. Helton's wages again, two dollars and a half a month each time.

"The man's worth it, Ellie," said Mr. Thompson, in a glow of self-justification for his extravagance. "He's made this place pay, and I want him to know I appreciate it."

Mr. Helton's silence, the pallor of his eyebrows and hair, his long, glum jaw and eyes that refused to see anything, even the work under his hands, had grown perfectly familiar to the Thompsons. At first, Mrs. Thompson complained a little. "It's like sitting down at the table with a disembodied spirit," she said. "You'd think he'd find something to say, sooner or later."

"Let him alone," said Mr. Thompson. "When he gets ready to talk, he'll talk."

The years passed, and Mr. Helton never got ready to

talk. After his work was finished for the day, he would come up from the barn or the milk house or the chicken house, swinging his lantern, his big shoes clumping like pony hoofs on the hard path. They, sitting in the kitchen in the winter, or on the back porch in summer, would hear him drag out his wooden chair, hear the creak of it tilted back, and then for a little while he would play his single tune on one or another of his harmonicas. The harmonicas were in different keys, some lower and sweeter than the others, but the same changeless tune went on, a strange tune, with sudden turns in it, night after night, and sometimes even in the afternoons when Mr. Helton sat down to catch his breath. At first the Thompsons liked it very much, and always stopped to listen. Later there came a time when they were fairly sick of it, and began to wish to each other that he would learn a new one. At last they did not hear it any more, it was as natural as the sound of the wind rising in the evenings, or the cows lowing, or their own voices.

Mrs. Thompson pondered now and then over Mr. Helton's soul. He didn't seem to be a church-goer, and worked straight through Sunday as if it were any common day of the week. "I think we ought to invite him to go to hear Dr. Martin," she told Mr. Thompson. "It isn't very Christian of us not to ask him. He's not a forward kind of man. He'd wait to be asked."

"Let him alone," said Mr. Thompson. "The way I look at it, his religion is every man's own business. Besides, he ain't got any Sunday clothes. He wouldn't want to go to church in them jeans and jumpers of his. I don't know what he does with his money. He certainly don't spend it foolishly."

Still, once the notion got into her head, Mrs. Thompson could not rest until she invited Mr. Helton to go to church with the family next Sunday. He was pitching hay into neat little piles in the field back of the orchard. Mrs. Thompson put on smoked glasses and a sunbonnet and walked all the way down there to speak to him. He stopped and leaned on his pitchfork, listening, and for a moment Mrs. Thompson was almost frightened at his face. The pale eyes seemed to glare past her, the eyebrows frowned, the long jaw hardened. "I got work," he said bluntly, and lifting his pitchfork he turned from her and began to toss the hay. Mrs. Thompson, her feelings hurt, walked back thinking that by now she should be used to Mr. Helton's ways, but it did seem like a man, even a foreigner, could be just a little polite when you gave him a Christian invitation. "He's not polite, that's the only thing I've got against him," she said to Mr. Thompson. "He just can't seem to behave like other people. You'd think he had a grudge against the world," she said. "I sometimes don't know what to make of it."

In the second year something had happened that made Mrs. Thompson uneasy, the kind of thing she could not put into words, hardly into thoughts, and if she had tried to explain to Mr. Thompson it would have sounded worse than it was, or not bad enough. It was that kind of queer thing that seems to be giving a warning, and yet, nearly always nothing comes of it. It was on a hot, still spring day, and Mrs. Thompson had been down to the garden patch to pull some new carrots and green onions and string beans for dinner. As she worked, sunbonnet low over her eyes, putting each kind of vegetable in a pile by itself in her basket, she noticed how neatly Mr. Helton weeded, and how rich the soil was. He had spread it all over with manure from the barns, and worked it in, in the fall, and the vegetables were coming up fine and full. She walked back under the nubbly little fig trees where the unpruned branches leaned almost to the ground, and the thick leaves made a cool screen. Mrs. Thompson was always looking for shade to save her eyes. So she, looking idly about, saw through the screen a sight that struck her as very strange. If it had been a noisy spectacle, it would have been quite natural. It was the silence that struck her. Mr. Helton was shaking Arthur by the shoulders, ferociously, his face most terribly fixed and pale. Arthur's head snapped back and forth and he had not stiffened in resistance, as he did when Mrs. Thompson tried to shake him. His eyes were rather frightened, but surprised, too, probably more surprised than anything else. Herbert stood by meekly, watching. Mr. Helton dropped Arthur, and seized Herbert, and shook him with the same methodical ferocity, the same face of hatred. Herbert's mouth crumpled as if he would cry, but he made no sound. Mr. Helton let him go, turned and strode into the shack, and the little boys ran, as if for their lives, without a word. They disappeared around the corner to the front of the house.

Mrs. Thompson took time to set her basket on the kitchen table, to push her sunbonnet back on her head and draw it forward again, to look in the stove and make certain the fire was going, before she followed the boys. They were sitting huddled together under a clump of chinaberry trees in plain sight of her bedroom window, as if it were a safe place they had discovered.

"What are you doing?" asked Mrs. Thompson.

They looked hang-dog from under their foreheads and Arthur mumbled, "Nothin'."

"Nothing *now*, you mean," said Mrs. Thompson, severely. "Well, I have plenty for you to do. Come right in here this minute and help me fix vegetables. This minute."

They scrambled up very eagerly and followed her close. Mrs. Thompson tried to imagine what they had been up to; she did not like the notion of Mr. Helton taking it on himself to correct her little boys, but she was afraid to ask them for reasons. They might tell her a lie, and she would have to overtake them in it, and whip them. Or she would have to pretend to believe them, and they would get in the habit of lying. Or they might tell her the truth, and it would be something she would have to whip them for. The very thought of it gave her a headache. She supposed she might ask Mr. Helton, but it was not her place to ask. She would wait and tell Mr. Thompson, and let him get at the bottom of it. While her mind ran on, she kept the little boys hopping. "Cut those carrot tops closer, Herbert, you're just being careless. Arthur, stop breaking up the beans so little. They're little enough already. Herbert, you go get an armload of wood. Arthur, you take these onions and wash them under the pump. Herbert, as soon as you're done here, you get a broom and sweep out this kitchen. Arthur, you get a shovel and take up the ashes. Stop picking your nose, Herbert. How often must I tell you? Arthur, you go look in the top drawer of my bureau, left-hand side, and bring me the vaseline for Herbert's nose. Herbert, come here to me. . . ."

They galloped through their chores, their animal spirits rose with activity, and shortly they were out in the front yard again, engaged in a wrestling match. They sprawled and fought, scrambled, clutched, rose and fell shouting, as aimlessly, noisily, monotonously as two puppies. They imitated various animals, not a human sound from them, and their dirty faces were streaked with sweat. Mrs. Thompson, sitting at her window, watched them with baffled pride and tenderness, they were so sturdy and healthy and growing so fast; but uneasily, too, with her pained little smile and the tears rolling from her eyelids that clinched themselves against the sunlight. They were so idle and careless, as if they had no future in this world, and no immortal souls to save, and oh, what had they been up to that Mr. Helton had shaken them, with his face positively dangerous?

In the evening before supper, without a word to Mr. Thompson of the curious fear the sight had caused her, she told him that Mr. Helton had shaken the little boys for some reason. He stepped out to the shack and spoke to Mr. Helton. In five minutes he was back, glaring at his young. "He says them brats been fooling with his harmonicas, Ellie, blowing in them and getting them all dirty and full of spit and they don't play good."

"Did he say all that?" asked Mrs. Thompson. "It doesn't seem possible."

"Well, that's what he meant, anyhow," said Mr. Thompson. "He didn't say it just that way. But he acted pretty worked up about it."

"That's a shame," said Mrs. Thompson, "a perfect shame. Now we've got to do something so they'll remember they mustn't go into Mr. Helton's things."

"I'll tan their hides for them," said Mr. Thompson. "I'll take a calf rope to them if they don't look out."

"Maybe you'd better leave the whipping to me," said Mrs. Thompson. "You haven't got a light enough hand for children."

"That's just what's the matter with them now," shouted Mr. Thompson, "rotten spoiled and they'll wind up in the penitentiary. You don't half whip 'em. Just little love taps. My pa used to knock me down with a stick of stove wood or anything else that came handy."

"Well, that's not saying it's right," said Mrs. Thompson. "I don't hold with that way of raising children. It makes them run away from home. I've seen too much of it."

"I'll break every bone in 'em," said Mr. Thompson, simmering down, "if they don't mind you better and stop being so bull-headed."

"Leave the table and wash your face and hands," Mrs. Thompson commanded the boys, suddenly. They slunk out and dabbled at the pump and slunk in again, trying to make themselves small. They had learned long ago that their mother always made them wash when there was trouble ahead. They looked at their plates. Mr. Thompson opened up on them.

"Well, now, what you got to say for yourselves about going into Mr. Helton's shack and ruining his harmonicas?"

The two little boys wilted, their faces drooped into the grieved hopeless lines of children's faces when they are brought to the terrible bar of blind adult justice; their eyes telegraphed each other in panic, "Now we're really going to catch a licking"; in despair, they dropped their buttered cornbread on their plates, their hands lagged on the edge of the table.

"I ought to break your ribs," said Mr. Thompson, "and I'm a good mind to do it."

"Yes, sir," whispered Arthur, faintly.

"Yes, sir," said Herbert, his lip trembling.

"Now, papa," said Mrs. Thompson in a warning tone. The children did not glance at her. They had no faith in her good will. She had betrayed them in the first place. There was no trusting her. Now she might save them and she might not. No use depending on her.

"Well, you ought to get a good thrashing. You deserve it, don't you, Arthur?"

Arthur hung his head. "Yes, sir."

"And the next time I catch either of you hanging around Mr. Helton's shack, I'm going to take the hide off *both* of you, you hear me, Herbert?"

Herbert mumbled and choked, scattering his cornbread. "Yes, sir."

"Well, now sit up and eat your supper and not another word out of you," said Mr. Thompson, beginning on his own food. The little boys perked up somewhat and started chewing, but every time they looked around they met their parents' eyes, regarding them steadily. There was no telling when they would think of something new. The boys ate warily, trying not to be seen or heard, the cornbread sticking, the buttermilk gurgling, as it went down their gullets.

"And something else, Mr. Thompson," said Mrs. Thompson after a pause. "Tell Mr. Helton he's to come straight to us when they bother him, and not to trouble shaking them himself. Tell him we'll look after that."

"They're so mean," answered Mr. Thompson, staring at them. "It's a wonder he don't just kill 'em off and be done with it." But there was something in the tone that told Arthur and Herbert that nothing more worth worrying about was going to happen this time. Heaving deep sighs, they sat up, reaching for the food nearest them.

"Listen," said Mrs. Thompson, suddenly. The little

boys stopped eating. "Mr. Helton hasn't come for his supper. Arthur, go and tell Mr. Helton he's late for supper. Tell him nice, now."

Arthur, miserably depressed, slid out of his place and made for the door, without a word.

There were no miracles of fortune to be brought to pass on a small dairy farm. The Thompsons did not grow rich, but they kept out of the poor house, as Mr. Thompson was fond of saying, meaning he had got a little foothold in spite of Ellie's poor health, and unexpected weather, and strange declines in market prices, and his own mysterious handicaps which weighed him down. Mr. Helton was the hope and the prop of the family, and all the Thompsons became fond of him, or at any rate they ceased to regard him as in any way peculiar, and looked upon him, from a distance they did not know how to bridge, as a good man and a good friend. Mr. Helton went his way, worked, played his tune. Nine years passed. The boys grew up and learned to work. They could not remember the time when Ole Helton hadn't been there: a grouchy cuss, Brother Bones; Mr. Helton, the dairymaid; that Big Swede. If he had heard them, he might have been annoyed at some of the names they called him. But he did not hear them, and besides they meant no harm—or at least such harm as existed was all there, in the names; the boys referred to their father as the Old Man, or the Old Geezer, but not to his face. They lived through by main strength all the grimy, secret, oblique phases of growing up and got past the crisis safely if anyone does. Their parents could see they were good solid boys with hearts of gold in spite of their rough ways. Mr. Thompson was relieved to find

that, without knowing how he had done it, he had suc-
ceeded in raising a set of boys who were not trifling
whittlers. They were such good boys Mr. Thompson
began to believe they were born that way, and that he
had never spoken a harsh word to them in their lives,
much less thrashed them. Herbert and Arthur never dis-
puted his word.

Mr. Helton, his hair wet with sweat, plastered to his
dripping forehead, his jumper streaked dark and light
blue and clinging to his ribs, was chopping a little firewood. He chopped slowly, struck the ax into the end
of the chopping log, and piled the wood up neatly. He
then disappeared round the house into his shack, which
shared with the wood pile a good shade from a row of
mulberry trees. Mr. Thompson was lolling in a swing
chair on the front porch, a place he had never liked. The
chair was new, and Mrs. Thompson had wanted it on
the front porch, though the side porch was the place for
it, being cooler; and Mr. Thompson wanted to sit in the
chair, so there he was. As soon as the new wore off of
it, and Ellie's pride in it was exhausted, he would move
it round to the side porch. Meantime the August heat
was almost unbearable, the air so thick you could poke
a hole in it. The dust was inches thick on everything,
though Mr. Helton sprinkled the whole yard regularly
every night. He even shot the hose upward and washed
the tree tops and the roof of the house. They had laid
waterpipes to the kitchen and an outside faucet. Mr.
Thompson must have dozed, for he opened his eyes and
shut his mouth just in time to save his face before a
stranger who had driven up to the front gate. Mr.
Thompson stood up, put on his hat, pulled up his jeans,

and watched while the stranger tied his team, attached to a light spring wagon, to the hitching post. Mr. Thompson recognized the team and wagon. They were from a livery stable in Buda. While the stranger was opening the gate, a strong gate that Mr. Helton had built and set firmly on its hinges several years back, Mr. Thompson strolled down the path to greet him and find out what in God's world a man's business might be that would bring him out at this time of day, in all this dust and welter.

He wasn't exactly a fat man. He was more like a man who had been fat recently. His skin was baggy and his clothes were too big for him, and he somehow looked like a man who should be fat, ordinarily, but who might have just got over a spell of sickness. Mr. Thompson didn't take to his looks at all, he couldn't say why.

The stranger took off his hat. He said in a loud hearty voice, "Is this Mr. Thompson, Mr. Royal Earle Thompson?"

"That's my name," said Mr. Thompson, almost quietly, he was so taken aback by the free manner of the stranger.

"My name is Hatch," said the stranger, "Mr. Homer T. Hatch, and I've come to see you about buying a horse."

"I reckon you've been misdirected," said Mr. Thompson. "I haven't got a horse for sale. Usually if I've got anything like that to sell," he said, "I tell the neighbors and tack up a little sign on the gate."

The fat man opened his mouth and roared with joy, showing rabbit teeth brown as shoeleather. Mr. Thompson saw nothing to laugh at, for once. The stranger shouted, "That's just an old joke of mine." He caught one of his hands in the other and shook hands with himself heartily, "I always say something like that when I'm calling on a stranger, because I've noticed that when a feller says he's come to buy something nobody takes him for a suspicious character. You see? Haw, haw, haw."

His joviality made Mr. Thompson nervous, because the expression in the man's eyes didn't match the sounds he was making. "Haw, haw," laughed Mr. Thompson obligingly, still not seeing the joke. "Well, that's all wasted on me because I never take any man for a suspicious character 'til he shows hisself to be one. Says or does something," he explained. "Until that happens, one man's as good as another, so far's *I'm* concerned."

"Well," said the stranger, suddenly very sober and sensible, "I ain't come neither to buy nor sell. Fact is, I want to see you about something that's of interest to us both. Yes, sir, I'd like to have a little talk with you, and it won't cost you a cent."

"I guess that's fair enough," said Mr. Thompson, reluctantly. "Come on around the house where there's a little shade."

They went round and seated themselves on two stumps under a chinaberry tree.

"Yes, sir, Homer T. Hatch is my name and America is my nation," said the stranger. "I reckon you must know the name? I used to have a cousin named Jameson Hatch lived up the country a ways."

"Don't think I know the name," said Mr. Thompson. "There's some Hatchers settled somewhere around Mountain City."

"Don't know the old Hatch family," cried the man in deep concern. He seemed to be pitying Mr. Thompson's ignorance. "Why, we came over from Georgia fifty years ago. Been here long yourself?"

"Just all my whole life," said Mr. Thompson, beginning to feel peevish. "And my pa and my grampap before me. Yes, sir, we've been right here all along. Anybody wants to find a Thompson knows where to look for him. My grampap immigrated in 1836."

"From Ireland, I reckon?" said the stranger.

"From Pennsylvania," said Mr. Thompson. "Now what makes you think we came from Ireland?"

The stranger opened his mouth and began to shout with merriment, and he shook hands with himself as if he hadn't met himself for a long time. "Well, what I always says is, a feller's got to come from *somewhere*, ain't he?"

While they were talking, Mr. Thompson kept glancing at the face near him. He certainly did remind Mr. Thompson of somebody, or maybe he really had seen the man himself somewhere. He couldn't just place the features. Mr. Thompson finally decided it was just that all rabbit-teethed men looked alike.

"That's right," acknowledged Mr. Thompson, rather sourly, "but what I always say is, Thompsons have been settled here for so long it don't make much difference any more *where* they come from. Now a course, this is the slack season, and we're all just laying round a little, but nevertheless we've all got our chores to do, and I don't want to hurry you, and so if you've come to see me on business maybe we'd better get down to it."

"As I said, it's not in a way, and again in a way it is," said the fat man. "Now I'm looking for a man named Helton, Mr. Olaf Eric Helton, from North Dakota, and

I was told up around the country a ways that I might find him here, and I wouldn't mind having a little talk with him. No, siree, I sure wouldn't mind, if it's all the same to you."

"I never knew his middle name," said Mr. Thompson, "but Mr. Helton is right here, and been here now for going on nine years. He's a mighty steady man, and you can tell anybody I said so."

"I'm glad to hear that," said Mr. Homer T. Hatch. "I like to hear of a feller mending his ways and settling down. Now when I knew Mr. Helton he was pretty wild, yes, sir, wild is what he was, he didn't know his own mind atall. Well, now, it's going to be a great pleasure to me to meet up with an old friend and find him all settled down and doing well by hisself."

"We've all got to be young once," said Mr. Thompson. "It's like the measles, it breaks out all over you, and you're a nuisance to yourself and everybody else, but it don't last, and it usually don't leave no ill effects." He was so pleased with this notion he forgot and broke into a guffaw. The stranger folded his arms over his stomach and went into a kind of fit, roaring until he had tears in his eyes. Mr. Thompson stopped shouting and eyed the stranger uneasily. Now he liked a good laugh as well as any man, but there ought to be a little moderation. Now this feller laughed like a perfect lunatic, that was a fact. And he wasn't laughing because he really thought things were funny, either. He was laughing for reasons of his own. Mr. Thompson fell into a moody silence, and waited until Mr. Hatch settled down a little.

Mr. Hatch got out a very dirty blue cotton bandanna and wiped his eyes. "That joke just about caught me where I live," he said, almost apologetically. "Now I wish I could think up things as funny as that to say. It's a gift. It's . . ."

"If you want to speak to Mr. Helton, I'll go and round him up," said Mr. Thompson, making motions as if he might get up. "He may be in the milk house and he may be setting in his shack this time of day." It was drawing towards five o'clock. "It's right around the corner," he said.

"Oh, well, there ain't no special hurry," said Mr. Hatch. "I've been wanting to speak to him for a good long spell now and I guess a few minutes more won't make no difference. I just more wanted to locate him, like. That's all."

Mr. Thompson stopped beginning to stand up, and unbuttoned one more button of his shirt, and said, "Well, he's here, and he's this kind of man, that if he had any business with you he'd like to get it over. He don't dawdle, that's one thing you can say for him."

Mr. Hatch appeared to sulk a little at these words. He wiped his face with the bandanna and opened his mouth to speak, when round the house there came the music of Mr. Helton's harmonica. Mr. Thompson raised a finger. "There he is," said Mr. Thompson. "Now's your time."

Mr. Hatch cocked an ear towards the east side of the house and listened for a few seconds, a very strange expression on his face.

"I know that tune like I know the palm of my own hand," said Mr. Thompson, "but I never heard Mr. Helton say what it was."

"That's a kind of Scandahoovian song," said Mr. Hatch. "Where I come from they sing it a lot. In North

Dakota, they sing it. It says something about starting out in the morning feeling so good you can't hardly stand it, so you drink up all your likker before noon. All the likker, y' understand, that you was saving for the noon lay-off. The words ain't much, but it's a pretty tune. It's a kind of drinking song." He sat there drooping a little, and Mr. Thompson didn't like his expression. It was a satisfied expression, but it was more like the cat that et the canary.

"So far as I know," said Mr. Thompson, "he ain't touched a drop since he's been on the place, and that's nine years this coming September. Yes, sir, nine years, so far as I know, he ain't wetted his whistle once. And that's more than I can say for myself," he said, meekly proud.

"Yes, that's a drinking song," said Mr. Hatch. "I used to play 'Little Brown Jug' on the fiddle when I was younger than I am now," he went on, "but this Helton, he just keeps it up. He just sits and plays it by himself."

"He's been playing it off and on for nine years right here on the place," said Mr. Thompson, feeling a little proprietary.

"And he was certainly singing it as well, fifteen years before that, in North Dakota," said Mr. Hatch. "He used to sit up in a straitjacket, practically, when he was in the asylum—"

"What's that you say?" said Mr. Thompson. "What's that?"

"Shucks, I didn't mean to tell you," said Mr. Hatch, a faint leer of regret in his drooping eyelids. "Shucks, that just slipped out. Funny, now I'd made up my mind I wouldn't say a word, because it would just make a lot of excitement, and what I say is, if a man has lived harmless and quiet for nine years it don't matter if he *is* loony, does it? So long's he keeps quiet and don't do nobody harm."

"You mean they had him in a straitjacket?" asked Mr. Thompson, uneasily. "In a lunatic asylum?"

"They sure did," said Mr. Hatch. "That's right where they had him, from time to time."

"They put my Aunt Ida in one of them things in the State asylum," said Mr. Thompson. "She got vi'lent, and they put her in one of these jackets with long sleeves and tied her to an iron ring in the wall, and Aunt Ida got so wild she broke a blood vessel and when they went to look after her she was dead. I'd think one of them things was dangerous."

"Mr. Helton used to sing his drinking song when he was in a straitjacket," said Mr. Hatch. "Nothing ever bothered him, except if you tried to make him talk. That bothered him, and he'd get vi'lent, like your Aunt Ida. He'd get vi'lent and then they'd put him in the jacket and go off and leave him, and he'd lay there perfickly contented, so far's you could see, singing his song. Then one night he just disappeared. Left, you might say, just went, and nobody ever saw hide or hair of him again. And then I come along and find him here," said Mr. Hatch, "all settled down and playing the same song."

"He never acted crazy to me," said Mr. Thompson. "He always acted like a sensible man, to me. He never got married, for one thing, and he works like a horse, and I bet he's got the first cent I paid him when he landed here, and he don't drink, and he never says a word, much less swear, and he don't waste time runnin' around Saturday nights, and if he's crazy," said Mr. Thompson, "why, I think I'll go crazy myself for a change."

"Haw, ha," said Mr. Hatch, "heh, he, that's good! Ha, ha, ha, I hadn't thought of it jes like that. Yeah that's right! Let's all go crazy and get rid of our wives and save our money, hey?" He smiled unpleasantly, showing his little rabbit teeth.

Mr. Thompson felt he was being misunderstood. He turned around and motioned toward the open window back of the honeysuckle trellis. "Let's move off down here a little," he said. "I oughta thought of that before." His visitor bothered Mr. Thompson. He had a way of taking the words out of Mr. Thompson's mouth, turning them around and mixing them up until Mr. Thompson didn't know himself what he had said. "My wife's not very strong," said Mr. Thompson. "She's been kind of invalid now goin' on fourteen years. It's mighty tough on a poor man, havin' sickness in the family. She had four operations," he said proudly, "one right after the other, but they didn't do any good. For five years hand-runnin', I just turned every nickel I made over to the doctors. Upshot is, she's a mighty delicate woman."

"My old woman," said Mr. Homer T. Hatch, "had a back like a mule, yes, sir. That woman could have moved the barn with her bare hands if she'd ever took the notion. I used to say, it was a good thing she didn't know her own stren'th. She's dead now, though. That kind wear out quicker than the puny ones. I never had much use for a woman always complainin'. I'd get rid of her mighty quick, yes, sir, mighty quick. It's just as you say: a dead loss, keepin' one of 'em up."

This was not at all what Mr. Thompson had heard himself say; he had been trying to explain that a wife as expensive as his was a credit to a man. "She's a mighty reasonable woman," said Mr. Thompson, feeling baffled, "but I wouldn't answer for what she'd say or do if she found out we'd had a lunatic on the place all this time." They had moved away from the window; Mr. Thompson took Mr. Hatch the front way, because if he went the back way they would have to pass Mr. Helton's shack. For some reason he didn't want the stranger to see or talk to Mr. Helton. It was strange, but that was the way Mr. Thompson felt.

Mr. Thompson sat down again, on the chopping log, offering his guest another tree stump. "Now, I mighta got upset myself at such a thing, once," said Mr. Thompson, "but now I *deefy* anything to get me lathered up." He cut himself an enormous plug of tobacco with his horn-handled pocketknife, and offered it to Mr. Hatch, who then produced his own plug and, opening a huge bowie knife with a long blade sharply whetted, cut off a large wad and put it in his mouth. They then compared plugs and both of them were astonished to see how different men's ideas of good chewing tobacco were.

"Now, for instance," said Mr. Hatch, "mine is lighter colored. That's because, for one thing, there ain't any sweetenin' in this plug. I like it dry, natural leaf, medium strong."

"A little sweetenin' don't do no harm so far as I'm concerned," said Mr. Thompson, "but it's got to be mighty little. But with me, now, I want a strong leaf, I want it heavy-cured, as the feller says. There's a man near here, named Williams, Mr. John Morgan Williams, who chews a plug—well, sir, it's black as your hat and soft as melted tar. It fairly drips with molasses, jus' plain molasses, and it chews like licorice. Now, I don't call that a good chew."

"One man's meat," said Mr. Hatch, "is another man's

poison. Now, such a chew would simply gag me. I couldn't begin to put it in my mouth."

"Well," said Mr. Thompson, a tinge of apology in his voice, "I jus' barely tasted it myself, you might say. Just took a little piece in my mouth and spit it out again."

"I'm dead sure I couldn't even get that far," said Mr. Hatch. "I like a dry natural chew without any artificial flavorin' of any kind."

Mr. Thompson began to feel that Mr. Hatch was trying to make out he had the best judgment in tobacco, and was going to keep up the argument until he proved it. He began to feel seriously annoyed with the fat man. After all, who was he and where did he come from? Who was he to go around telling other people what kind of tobacco to chew?

"Artificial flavorin'," Mr. Hatch went on, doggedly, "is jes put in to cover up a cheap leaf and make a man think he's gettin' somethin' more than he *is* gettin'. Even a little sweetenin' is a sign of a cheap leaf, you can mark my words."

"I've always paid a fair price for my plug," said Mr. Thompson, stiffly. "I'm not a rich man and I don't go round settin' myself up for one, but I'll say this, when it comes to such things as tobacco, I buy the best on the market."

"Sweetenin', even a little," began Mr. Hatch, shifting his plug and squirting tobacco juice at a dry-looking little rose bush that was having a hard enough time as it was, standing all day in the blazing sun, its roots clenched in the baked earth, "is the sign of—"

"About this Mr. Helton, now," said Mr. Thompson, determinedly, "I don't see no reason to hold it against a man because he went loony once or twice in his lifetime and so I don't expect to take no steps about it. Not a step. I've got nothin' against the man, he's always treated me fair. They's things and people," he went on, "'nough to drive any man loony. The wonder to me is, more men don't wind up in straitjackets, the way things are going these days and times."

"That's right," said Mr. Hatch, promptly, entirely too promptly, as if he were turning Mr. Thompson's meaning back on him. "You took the words right out of my mouth. There ain't every man in a straitjacket that ought to be there. Ha, ha, you're right all right. You got the idea."

Mr. Thompson sat silent and chewed steadily and stared at a spot on the ground about six feet away and felt a slow muffled resentment climbing from somewhere deep down in him, climbing and spreading all through him. What was this fellow driving at? What was he trying to say? It wasn't so much his words, but his looks and his way of talking: that droopy look in the eye, that tone of voice, as if he was trying to mortify Mr. Thompson about something. Mr. Thompson didn't like it, but he couldn't get hold of it either. He wanted to turn around and shove the fellow off the stump, but it wouldn't look reasonable. Suppose something happened to the fellow when he fell off the stump, just for instance, if he fell on the ax and cut himself, and then someone should ask Mr. Thompson why he shoved him, and what could a man say? It would look mighty funny, it would sound mighty strange to say, Well, him and me fell out over a plug of tobacco. He might just shove him anyhow and then tell people he was a fat man not used to the heat and while he was talking he got dizzy and fell off by himself, or something like that, and it wouldn't be the truth either, because it wasn't the heat and it wasn't the tobacco. Mr. Thompson made up his mind to get the fellow off the place pretty quick, without seeming to be anxious, and watch him sharp till he was out of sight. It doesn't pay to be friendly with strangers from another part of the country. They're always up to something, or they'd stay at home where they belong.

"And they's some people," said Mr. Hatch, "would jus' as soon have a loonatic around their house as not, they can't see no difference between them and anybody else. I always say, if that's the way a man feels, don't care who he associates with, why, why, that's his business, not mine. I don't wanta have a thing to do with it. Now back home in North Dakota, we don't feel that way. I'd like to a seen anybody hiring a loonatic there, especially after what he done."

"I didn't understand your home was North Dakota," said Mr. Thompson. "I thought you said Georgia."

"I've got a married sister in North Dakota," said Mr. Hatch, "married a Swede, but a white man if ever I saw one. So I say *we* because we got into a little business together out that way. And it seems like home, kind of."

"What did he do?" asked Mr. Thompson, feeling very uneasy again.

"Oh, nothin' to speak of," said Mr. Hatch, jovially, "jus' went loony one day in the hayfield and shoved a pitchfork right square through his brother, when they was makin' hay. They was goin' to execute him, but they found out he had went crazy with the heat, as the feller says, and so they put him in the asylum. That's all he done. Nothin' to get lathered up about, ha, ha, ha!" he said, and taking out his sharp knife he began to slice off a chew as carefully as if he were cutting cake.

"Well," said Mr. Thompson, "I don't deny that's news. Yes, sir, news. But I still say somethin' must have drove him to it. Some men make you feel like giving 'em a good killing just by lookin' at you. His brother may a been a mean ornery cuss."

"Brother was going to get married," said Mr. Hatch; "used to go courtin' his girl nights. Borrowed Mr. Helton's harmonica to give her a serenade one evenin', and lost it. Brand new harmonica."

"He thinks a heap of his harmonicas," said Mr. Thompson. "Only money he ever spends, now and then he buys hisself a new one. Must have a dozen in that shack, all kinds and sizes."

"Brother wouldn't buy him a new one," said Mr. Hatch, "so Mr. Helton just ups, as I says, and runs his pitchfork through his brother. Now you know he musta been crazy to get all worked up over a little thing like that."

"Sounds like it," said Mr. Thompson, reluctant to agree in anything with this intrusive and disagreeable fellow. He kept thinking he couldn't remember when he had taken such a dislike to a man on first sight.

"Seems to me you'd get pretty sick of hearin' the same tune year in, year out," said Mr. Hatch.

"Well, sometimes I think it wouldn't do no harm if he learned a new one," said Mr. Thompson, "but he don't, so there's nothin' to be done about it. It's a pretty good tune, though."

"One of the Scandahoovians told me what it meant, that's how I come to know," said Mr. Hatch. "Especially that part about getting so gay you jus' go ahead and drink up all the likker you got on hand before noon. It seems like up in them Swede countries a man carries a bottle of wine around with him as a matter of course, at least that's the way I understood it. Those fellers will tell you anything, though—" He broke off and spat.

The idea of drinking any kind of liquor in this heat made Mr. Thompson dizzy. The idea of anybody feeling good on a day like this, for instance, made him tired. He felt he was really suffering from the heat. The fat man looked as if he had grown to the stump; he slumped there in his damp, dark clothes too big for him, his belly slack in his pants, his wide black felt hat pushed off his narrow forehead red with prickly heat. A bottle of good cold beer, now, would be a help, thought Mr. Thompson, remembering the four bottles sitting deep in the pool at the springhouse, and his dry tongue squirmed in his mouth. He wasn't going to offer this man anything, though, not even a drop of water. He wasn't even going to chew any more tobacco with him. He shot out his quid suddenly, and wiped his mouth on the back of his hand, and studied the head near him attentively. The man was no good, and he was there for no good, but what was he up to? Mr. Thompson made up his mind he'd give him a little more time to get his business, whatever it was, with Mr. Helton over, and then if he didn't get off the place he'd kick him off.

Mr. Hatch, as if he suspected Mr. Thompson's thoughts, turned his eyes, wicked and pig-like, on Mr. Thompson. "Fact is," he said, as if he had made up his mind about something, "I might need your help in the little matter I've got on hand, but it won't cost you any trouble. Now, this Mr. Helton here, like I tell you, he's a dangerous escaped loonatic, you might say. Now fact is, in the last twelve years or so I musta rounded up twenty-odd escaped loonatics, besides a couple of escaped convicts that I just run into by accident, like. I don't make a business of it, but if there's a reward, and there usually is a reward, of course, I get it. It amounts to a tidy little sum in the long run, but that ain't the main question. Fact is, I'm for law and order, I don't like to see lawbreakers and loonatics at large. It ain't the place for them. Now I reckon you're bound to agree with me on that, aren't you?"

Mr. Thompson said, "Well, circumstances alters cases, as the feller says. Now, what I know of Mr. Helton, he ain't dangerous, as I told you." Something serious was going to happen, Mr. Thompson could see that. He stopped thinking about it. He'd just let this fellow shoot off his head and then see what could be done about it. Without thinking he got out his knife and plug and started to cut a chew, then remembered himself and put them back in his pocket.

"The law," said Mr. Hatch, "is solidly behind me. Now this Mr. Helton, he's been one of my toughest cases. He's kept my record from being practically one hundred per cent. I knew him before he went loony, and I know the fam'ly, so I undertook to help out rounding him up. Well, sir, he was gone slick as a whistle, for all we knew the man was as good as dead long while ago. Now we never might have caught up with him, but do you know what he did? Well, sir, about two weeks ago his old mother gets a letter from him, and in that letter, what do you reckon she found? Well, it was a check on that little bank in town for eight hundred and fifty dollars, just like that; the letter wasn't nothing much, just said he was sending her a few little savings, she might need something, but there it was, name, postmark, date, everything. The old woman practically lost her mind with joy. She's gettin' childish, and it looked like she kinda forgot that her only living son killed his brother and went loony. Mr. Helton said he was getting along all right, and for her not to tell nobody. Well, natchally, she couldn't keep it to herself, with that check to cash and everything. So that's how I come to know." His feelings got the better of him. "You coulda knocked me down with a feather." He shook hands with himself and rocked, wagging his head, going "Heh, heh," in his throat. Mr. Thompson felt the corners of his mouth turning down. Why, the dirty low-down hound, sneaking around spying into other people's business like that. Collecting blood money, that's what it was! Let him talk!

"Yea, well, that musta been a surprise all right," he said, trying to hold his voice even. "I'd say a surprise."

"Well, siree," said Mr. Hatch, "the more I got to thinking about it, the more I just come to the conclusion that I'd better look into the matter a little, and so I talked to the old woman. She's pretty decrepit, now, half blind and all, but she was all for taking the first train out and going to see her son. I put it up to her square—how she was too feeble for the trip, and all. So, just as a favor to her, I told her for my expenses I'd come down and see Mr. Helton and bring her back all the news about him. She gave me a new shirt she made herself by hand, and a big Swedish kind of cake to bring to him, but I musta mislaid them along the road somewhere. It don't reely matter, though, he prob'ly ain't in any state of mind to appreciate 'em."

Mr. Thompson sat up and turning round on the log looked at Mr. Hatch and asked as quietly as he could, "And now what are you aiming to do? That's the question."

Mr. Hatch slouched up to his feet and shook himself. "Well, I come all prepared for a little scuffle," he said. "I got the handcuffs," he said, "but I don't want no violence if I can help it. I didn't want to say nothing around the countryside, making an uproar. I figured the two of us could overpower him." He reached into his big inside pocket and pulled them out. Handcuffs, for God's sake, thought Mr. Thompson. Coming round on a peaceable afternoon worrying a man, and making trouble, and fishing handcuffs out of his pocket on a decent family homestead, as if it was all in the day's work.

Mr. Thompson, his head buzzing, got up too. "Well," he said, roundly, "I want to tell you I think you've got a mighty sorry job on hand, you sure must be hard up for something to do, and now I want to give you a good piece of advice. You just drop the idea that you're going to come here and make trouble for Mr. Helton, and the quicker you drive that hired rig away from my front gate the better I'll be satisfied."

Mr. Hatch put one handcuff in his outside pocket, the other dangling down. He pulled his hat down over his eyes, and reminded Mr. Thompson of a sheriff, somehow. He didn't seem in the least nervous, and didn't take up Mr. Thompson's words. He said, "Now listen just a minute, it ain't reasonable to suppose that a man like yourself is going to stand in the way of getting an escaped loonatic back to the asylum where he belongs. Now I know it's enough to throw you off, coming sudden like this, but fact is I counted on your being a respectable man and helping me out to see that justice is done. Now a course, if you won't help, I'll have to look around for help somewheres else. It won't look very good to your neighbors that you was harbring an escaped loonatic who killed his own brother, and then you refused to give him up. It will look mighty funny."

Mr. Thompson knew almost before he heard the words that it would look funny. It would put him in a mighty awkward position. He said, "But I've been trying to tell you all along that the man ain't loony now. He's been perfectly harmless for nine years. He's—he's—"

Mr. Thompson couldn't think how to describe how it was with Mr. Helton. "Why, he's been like one of the family," he said, "the best standby a man ever had." Mr. Thompson tried to see his way out. It was a fact Mr. Helton might go loony again any minute, and now this fellow talking around the country would put Mr. Thompson in a fix. It was a terrible position. He couldn't think of any way out. "You're crazy," Mr. Thompson roared suddenly, "you're the crazy one around here, you're crazier than he ever was! You get off this place or I'll handcuff you and turn you over to the law. You're tresspassing," shouted Mr. Thompson. "Get out of here before I knock you down!"

He took a step towards the fat man, who backed off, shrinking, "Try it, try it, go ahead!" and then something happened that Mr. Thompson tried hard afterwards to piece together in his mind, and in fact it never did come straight. He saw the fat man with his long bowie knife in his hand, he saw Mr. Helton come round the corner on the run, his long jaw dropped, his arms swinging, his eyes wild. Mr. Helton came in between them, fists doubled up, then stopped short, glaring at the fat man, his big frame seemed to collapse, he trembled like a shied horse; and then the fat man drove at him, knife in one hand, handcuffs in the other. Mr. Thompson saw it coming, he saw the blade going into Mr. Helton's stomache, he knew he had the ax out of the log in his own hands, felt his arms go up over his head and bring the ax down on Mr. Hatch's head as if he were stunning a beef.

Mrs. Thompson had been listening uneasily for some time to the voices going on, one of them strange to her, but she was too tired at first to get up and come out to see what was going on. The confused shouting that rose so suddenly brought her up to her feet and out across the front porch without her slippers, hair half-braided. Shading her eyes, she saw first Mr. Helton, running all stooped over through the orchard, running like a man with dogs after him; and Mr. Thompson supporting himself on the ax handle was leaning over shaking by the shoulder a man Mrs. Thompson had never seen, who lay doubled up with the top of his head smashed and the blood running away in a greasy-looking puddle. Mr. Thompson without taking his hand from the man's shoulder, said in a thick voice, "He killed Mr. Helton, he killed him, I saw him do it. I had to knock him out," he called loudly, "but he won't come to."

Mrs. Thompson said in a faint scream, "Why, yonder goes Mr. Helton," and she pointed. Mr. Thompson pulled himself up and looked where she pointed. Mrs. Thompson sat down slowly against the side of the house and began to slide forward on her face; she felt as if she were drowning, she couldn't rise to the top somehow, and her only thought was she was glad the boys were not there, they were out, fishing at Halifax, oh, God, she was glad the boys were not there.

Mr. and Mrs. Thompson drove up to their barn about sunset. Mr. Thompson handed the reins to his wife, got out to open the big door, and Mrs. Thompson guided old Jim in under the roof. The buggy was gray with dust and age, Mrs. Thompson's face was gray with dust and weariness, and Mr. Thompson's face, as he stood at the horse's head and began unhitching, was gray except for the dark blue of his freshly shaven jaws and chin, gray and blue and caved in, but patient, like a dead man's face.

Mrs. Thompson stepped down to the hard packed manure of the barn floor, and shook out her light flower-sprigged dress. She wore her smoked glasses, and her wide shady leghorn hat with the wreath of exhausted pink and blue forget-me-nots hid her forehead, fixed in a knot of distress.

The horse hung his head, raised a huge sigh and flexed his stiffened legs. Mr. Thompson's words came up muffled and hollow. "Poor ole Jim," he said, clearing his throat, "he looks pretty sunk in the ribs. I guess he's had a hard week." He lifted the harness up in one piece, slid it off and Jim walked out of the shafts halting a little. "Well, this is the last time," Mr. Thompson said, still talking to Jim. "Now you can get a good rest."

Mrs. Thompson closed her eyes behind her smoked glasses. The last time, and high time, and they should never have gone at all. She did not need her glasses any more, now the good darkness was coming down again, but her eyes ran full of tears steadily, though she was not crying, and she felt better with the glasses, safer, hidden away behind them. She took out her handkerchief with her hands shaking as they had been shaking ever since *that day*, and blew her nose. She said, "I see the boys have lighted the lamps. I hope they've started the stove going."

She stepped along the rough path holding her thin dress and starched petticoats around her, feeling her way between the sharp small stones, leaving the barn because she could hardly bear to be near Mr. Thompson, advancing slowly towards the house because she dreaded going there. Life was all one dread, the faces of her neighbors, of her boys, of her husband, the face of the whole world, the shape of her own house in the darkness, the very smell of the grass and the trees were horrible to her. There was no place to go, only one thing to do, bear it somehow—but how? She asked herself that question often. How was she going to keep on living now? Why had she lived at all? She wished now she had died one of those times when she had been so sick, instead of living on for this.

The boys were in the kitchen; Herbert was looking at the funny pictures from last Sunday's newspapers, the Katzenjammer Kids and Happy Hooligan. His chin was in his hands and his elbows on the table, and he was really reading and looking at the pictures, but his face was unhappy. Arthur was building the fire, adding kindling a stick at a time, watching it catch and blaze. His face was heavier and darker than Herbert's, but he was a little sullen by nature; Mrs. Thompson thought, he takes things harder, too. Arthur said, "Hello, Momma," and went on with his work. Herbert swept the papers together and moved over on the bench. They were big boys—fifteen and seventeen, and Arthur as tall as his father. Mrs. Thompson sat down beside Herbert, taking off her hat. She said, "I guess you're hungry. We were late today. We went the Log Hollow road, it's rougher than ever." Her pale mouth drooped with a sad fold on either side.

"I guess you saw the Mannings, then," said Herbert.

"Yes, and the Fergusons, and the Allbrights, and that new family McClellan."

"Anybody say anything?" asked Herbert.

"Nothing much, you know how it's been all along, some of them keeps saying, yes, they know it was a clear case and a fair trial and they say how glad they are your papa came out so well, and all that, some of 'em do, anyhow, but it looks like they don't really take sides with him. I'm about wore out," she said, the tears rolling again from under her dark glasses. "I don't know what good it does, but your papa can't seem to rest unless he's telling how it happened. I don't know."

"I don't think it does any good, not a speck," said Arthur, moving away from the stove. "It just keeps the whole question stirred up in people's minds. Everybody will go round telling what he heard, and the whole thing is going to get worse mixed up than ever. It just makes matters worse. I wish you could get Papa to stop driving round the country talking like that."

"Your papa knows best," said Mrs. Thompson. "You oughtn't to criticize him. He's got enough to put up with without that."

Arthur said nothing, his jaw stubborn. Mr. Thompson came in, his eyes hollowed out and dead-looking, his thick hands gray white and seamed from washing them clean every day before he started out to see the neighbors to tell them his side of the story. He was wearing his Sunday clothes, a thick pepper-and-salt-colored suit with a black string tie.

123

Mrs. Thompson stood up, her head swimming. "Now you-all get out of the kitchen, it's too hot in here and I need room. I'll get us a little bite of supper, if you'll just get out and give me some room."

They went as if they were glad to go, the boys outside, Mr. Thompson into his bedroom. She heard him groaning to himself as he took off his shoes, and heard the bed creak as he lay down. Mrs. Thompson opened the icebox and felt the sweet coldness flow out of it; she had never expected to have an icebox, much less did she hope to afford to keep it filled with ice. It still seemed like a miracle, after two or three years. There was the food, cold and clean, all ready to be warmed over. She would never have had that icebox if Mr. Helton hadn't happened along one day, just by the strangest luck; so saving, and so managing, so good, thought Mrs. Thompson, her heart swelling until she feared she would faint again, standing there with the door open and leaning her head upon it. She simply could not bear to remember Mr. Helton, with his long sad face and silent ways, who had always been so quiet and harmless, who had worked so hard and helped Mr. Thompson so much, running through the hot fields and woods, being hunted like a mad dog, everybody turning out with ropes and guns and sticks to catch and tie him. Oh, God, said Mrs. Thompson in a long dry moan, kneeling before the icebox and fumbling inside for the dishes, even if they did pile mattresses all over the jail floor and against the walls, and five men there to hold him to keep him from hurting himself any more, he was already hurt too badly, he couldn't have lived anyway. Mr. Barbee, the sheriff, told her about it. He said, well, they didn't aim to harm him but they had to catch him, he was crazy as a loon; he picked up rocks and tried to brain every man that got near him. He had two harmonicas in his jumper pocket, said the sheriff, but they fell out in the scuffle, and Mr. Helton tried to pick 'em up again, and that's when they finally got him. "They *had* to be rough, Miz Thompson, he fought like a wildcat." Yes, thought Mrs. Thompson again with the same bitterness, of course, they had to be rough. They always have to be rough. Mr. Thompson can't argue with a man and get him off the place peaceably; no, she thought, standing up and shutting the icebox, he has to kill somebody, he has to be a murderer and ruin his boys' lives and cause Mr. Helton to be killed like a mad dog.

Her thoughts stopped with a little soundless explosion, cleared and began again. The rest of Mr. Helton's harmonicas were still in the shack, his tune ran in Mrs. Thompson's head at certain times of the day. She missed it in the evenings. It seemed so strange she had never known the name of that song, nor what it meant, until after Mr. Helton was gone. Mrs. Thompson, trembling in the knees, took a drink of water at the sink and poured the red beans into the baking dish, and began to roll the pieces of chicken in flour to fry them. There was a time, she said to herself, when I thought I had neighbors and friends, there was a time when we could hold up our heads, there was a time when my husband hadn't killed a man and I could tell the truth to anybody about anything.

Mr. Thompson, turning on his bed, figured that he had done all he could, he'd just try to let the matter rest from now on. His lawyer, Mr. Burleigh, had told him right at the beginning, "Now you keep calm and collected. You've got a fine case, even if you haven't got witnesses. Your wife must sit in court, she'll be a powerful argument with the jury. You just plead not guilty and I'll do the rest. The trial is going to be a mere formality, you haven't got a thing to worry about. You'll be clean out of this before you know it." And to make talk Mr. Burleigh had got to telling about all the men he knew around the country who for one reason or another had been forced to kill somebody, always in self-defense, and there just wasn't anything to it at all. He even told about how his own father in the old days had shot and killed a man just for setting foot inside his gate when he told him not to. "Sure, I shot the scoundrel," said Mr. Burleigh's father, "in self-defense; I *told* him I'd shoot him if he set his foot in my yard, and he did, and I did." There had been bad blood between them for years, Mr. Burleigh said, and his father had waited a long time to catch the other fellow in the wrong, and when he did he certainly made the most of his opportunity.

"But Mr. Hatch, as I told you," Mr. Thompson had said, "made a pass at Mr. Helton with his bowie knife. That's why I took a hand."

"All the better," said Mr. Burleigh. "That stranger hadn't any right coming to your house on such an errand. Why, hell," said Mr. Burleigh, "that wasn't even manslaughter you committed. So now you just hold your horses and keep your shirt on. And don't say one word without I tell you."

Wasn't even manslaughter. Mr. Thompson had to cover Mr. Hatch with a piece of wagon canvas and ride to town to tell the sheriff. It had been hard on Ellie. When they got back, the sheriff and the coroner and two deputies, they found her sitting beside the road, on a low bridge over a gulley, about half a mile from the place. He had taken her up behind his saddle and got her back to the house. He had already told the sheriff that his wife had witnessed the whole business, and now he had time, getting her to her room and in bed, to tell her what to say if they asked anything. He had left out the part about Mr. Helton being crazy all along, but it came out at the trial. By Mr. Burleigh's advice Mr. Thompson had pretended to be perfectly ignorant; Mr. Hatch hadn't said a word about that. Mr. Thompson pretended to believe that Mr. Hatch had just come looking for Mr. Helton to settle old scores, and the two members of Mr. Hatch's family who had come down to try to get Mr. Thompson convicted didn't get anywhere at all. It hadn't been much of a trial, Mr. Burleigh saw to that. He had charged a reasonable fee, and Mr. Thompson had paid him and felt grateful, but after it was over Mr. Burleigh didn't seem pleased to see him when he got to dropping into the office to talk it over, telling him things that had slipped his mind at first: trying to explain what an ornery low hound Mr. Hatch had been, anyhow. Mr. Burleigh seemed to have lost his interest; he looked sour and upset when he saw Mr. Thompson at the door. Mr. Thompson kept saying to himself that he'd got off, all right, just as Mr. Burleigh had predicted, but, but—and it was right there that Mr. Thompson's mind stuck, squirming like an angleworm on a fishhook: he had killed Mr. Hatch, and he was a murderer. That was the truth about himself that Mr. Thompson couldn't grasp, even when he said the word to himself. Why, he had not even once *thought* of killing anybody, much less Mr. Hatch, and if Mr. Helton hadn't

come out so unexpectedly, hearing the row, why, then
—but then, Mr. Helton had come on the run that way
to help him. What he couldn't understand was what
happened next. He had seen Mr. Hatch go after Mr.
Helton with the knife, he had seen the point, blade up,
go into Mr. Helton's stomach and slice up like you slice
a hog, but when they finally caught Mr. Helton there
wasn't a knife scratch on him. Mr. Thompson knew he
had the ax in his own hands and felt himself lifting it,
but he couldn't remember hitting Mr. Hatch. He
couldn't remember it. He couldn't. He remembered only
that he had been determined to stop Mr. Hatch from
cutting Mr. Helton. If he was given a chance he could
explain the whole matter. At the trial they hadn't let him
talk. They just asked questions and he answered yes or
no, and they never did get to the core of the matter.
Since the trial, now, every day for a week he had washed
and shaved and put on his best clothes and had taken
Ellie with him to tell every neighbor he had that he never
killed Mr. Hatch on purpose, and what good did it do?
Nobody believed him. Even when he turned to Ellie and
said, "You was there, you saw it, didn't you?" and Ellie
spoke up, saying, "Yes, that's the truth. Mr. Thompson
was trying to save Mr. Helton's life," and he added, "If
you don't believe me, you can believe my wife. She won't
lie," Mr. Thompson saw something in all their faces that
disheartened him, made him feel empty and tired out.
They didn't believe he was not a murderer.

Even Ellie never said anything to comfort him. He
hoped she would say finally, "I remember now, Mr.
Thompson, I really did come round the corner in time
to see everything. It's not a lie, Mr. Thompson. Don't
you worry." But as they drove together in silence, with

the days still hot and dry, shortening for fall, day after
day, the buggy jolting in the ruts, she said nothing; they
grew to dread the sight of another house, and the people
in it: all houses looked alike now, and the people—old
neighbors or new—had the same expression when Mr.
Thompson told them why he had come and began his
story. Their eyes looked as if someone had pinched the
eyeball at the back; they shriveled and the light went out
of them. Some of them sat with fixed tight smiles trying
to be friendly. "Yes, Mr. Thompson, we know how you
must feel. It must be terrible for you, Mrs. Thompson.
Yes, you know, I've about come to the point where I
believe in such a thing as killing in self-defense. Why,
certainly, we believe you, Mr. Thompson, why
shouldn't we believe you? Didn't you have a perfectly
fair and above-board trial? Well, now, natchally, Mr.
Thompson, we think you done right."

Mr. Thompson was satisfied they didn't think so.
Sometimes the air around him was so thick with their
blame he fought and pushed with his fists, and the sweat
broke out all over him, he shouted his story in a dust-
choked voice, he would fairly bellow at last: "My wife,
here, you know her, she was there, she saw and heard
it all, if you don't believe me, ask her, she won't lie!"
and Mrs. Thompson, with her hands knotted together,
aching, her chin trembling, would never fail to say: "Yes,
that's right, that's the truth—"

The last straw had been laid on today, Mr. Thompson
decided. Tom Allbright, an old beau of Ellie's, why, he
had squired Ellie around a whole summer, had come out
to meet them when they drove up, and standing there
bareheaded had stopped them from getting out. He had
looked past them with an embarrassed frown on his face,

telling them his wife's sister was there with a raft of young ones, and the house was pretty full and everything upset, or he'd ask them to come in. "We've been thinking of trying to get up to your place one of these days," said Mr. Allbright, moving away trying to look busy, "we've been mighty occupied up here of late." So they had to say, "Well, we just happened to be driving this way," and go on. "The Allbrights," said Mrs. Thompson, "always was fair-weather friends." "They look out for number one, that's a fact," said Mr. Thompson. But it was cold comfort to them both.

Finally Mrs. Thompson had given up. "Let's go home," she said. "Old Jim's tired and thirsty, and we've gone far enough."

Mr. Thompson said, "Well, while we're out this way, we might as well stop at the McClellans'." They drove in, and asked a little cotton-haired boy if his mamma and papa were at home. Mr. Thompson wanted to see them. The little boy stood gazing with his mouth open, then galloped into the house shouting, "Mommer, Popper, come out hyah. That man that kilt Mr. Hatch has come ter see yer!"

The man came out in his sock feet, with one gallus up, the other broken and dangling, and said, "Light down, Mr. Thompson, and come in. The ole woman's washing, but she'll git here." Mrs. Thompson, feeling her way, stepped down and sat in a broken rocking-chair on the porch that sagged under her feet. The woman of the house, barefooted, in a calico wrapper, sat on the edge of the porch, her fat sallow face full of curiosity. Mr. Thompson began, "Well, as I reckon you happen to know, I've had some strange troubles lately, and, as the feller says, it's not the kind of trouble that happens

to a man every day in the year, and there's some things
I don't want no misunderstanding about in the neighbors' minds, so—" He halted and stumbled forward,
and the two listening faces took on a mean look, a
greedy, despising look, a look that said plain as day,
"My, you must be a purty sorry feller to come round
worrying about what *we* think, *we* know you wouldn't
be here if you had anybody else to turn to—my, I
wouldn't lower myself that much, myself." Mr. Thompson was ashamed of himself, he was suddenly in a rage,
he'd like to knock their dirty skunk heads together, the
low-down white trash—but he held himself down and
went on to the end. "My wife will tell you," he said,
and this was the hardest place, because Ellie always without moving a muscle seemed to stiffen as if somebody
had threatened to hit her; "ask my wife, she won't lie."

"It's true, I saw it—"

"Well, now," said the man, drily, scratching his ribs
inside his shirt, "that sholy is too bad. Well, now, I
kaint see what we've got to do with all this here, however. I kaint see no good reason for us to git mixed up
in these murder matters, I shore kaint. Whichever way
you look at it, it ain't none of my business. However,
it's mighty nice of you-all to come around and give us
the straight of it, fur we've heerd some mighty queer
yarns about it, mighty queer, I golly you couldn't hardly
make head ner tail of it."

"Evvybody goin' round shootin' they heads off," said
the woman. "Now we don't hold with killin'; the Bible
says—"

"Shet yer trap," said the man, "and keep it shet 'r I'll
shet it fer yer. Now it shore looks like to me—"

"We mustn't linger," said Mrs. Thompson, unclasping

her hands. "We've lingered too long now. It's getting late, and we've far to go." Mr. Thompson took the hint and followed her. The man and the woman lolled against their rickety porch poles and watched them go.

Now lying on his bed, Mr. Thompson knew the end had come. Now, this minute, lying in the bed where he had slept with Ellie for eighteen years; under this roof where he had laid the shingles when he was waiting to get married; there as he was with his whiskers already sprouting since his shave that morning; with his fingers feeling his bony chin, Mr. Thompson felt he was a dead man. He was dead to his other life, he had got to the end of something without knowing why, and he had to make a fresh start, he did not know how. Something different was going to begin, he didn't know what. It was in some way not his business. He didn't feel he was going to have much to do with it. He got up, aching, hollow, and went out to the kitchen where Mrs. Thompson was just taking up the supper.

"Call the boys," said Mrs. Thompson. They had been down to the barn, and Arthur put out the lantern before hanging it on a nail near the door. Mr. Thompson didn't like their silence. They had hardly said a word about anything to him since that day. They seemed to avoid him, they ran the place together as if he wasn't there, and attended to everything without asking him for any advice. "What you boys been up to?" he asked, trying to be hearty. "Finishing your chores?"

"No, sir," said Arthur, "there ain't much to do. Just greasing some axles." Herbert said nothing. Mrs. Thompson bowed her head: "For these and all Thy blessings. . . . Amen," she whispered weakly, and the

Thompsons sat there with their eyes down and their faces sorrowful, as if they were at a funeral.

Every time he shut his eyes, trying to sleep, Mr. Thompson's mind started up and began to run like a rabbit. It jumped from one thing to another, trying to pick up a trail here or there that would straighten out what had happened that day he killed Mr. Hatch. Try as he might, Mr. Thompson's mind would not go anywhere that it had not already been, he could not see anything but what he had seen once, and he knew that was not right. If he had not seen straight that first time, then everything about his killing Mr. Hatch was wrong from start to finish, and there was nothing more to be done about it, he might just as well give up. It still seemed to him that he had done, maybe not the right thing, but the only thing he could do, that day, but had he? *Did he have to kill Mr. Hatch?* He had never seen a man he hated more, the minute he laid eyes on him. He knew in his bones the fellow was there for trouble. What seemed so funny now was this: Why hadn't he just told Mr. Hatch to get out before he ever even got in?

Mrs. Thompson, her arms crossed on her breast, was lying beside him, perfectly still, but she seemed awake, somehow. "Asleep, Ellie?"

After all, he might have got rid of him peaceably, or maybe he might have had to overpower him and put those handcuffs on him and turn him over to the sheriff for disturbing the peace. The most they could have done was to lock Mr. Hatch up while he cooled off for a few days, or fine him a little something. He would try to think of things he might have said to Mr. Hatch. Why,

let's see, I could just have said, Now look here, Mr.
Hatch, I want to talk to you as man to man. But his
brain would go empty. What could he have said or done?
But if he *could* have done anything else almost except
kill Mr. Hatch, then nothing would have happened to
Mr. Helton. Mr. Thompson hardly ever thought of Mr.
Helton. His mind just skipped over him and went on.
If he stopped to think about Mr. Helton he'd never in
God's world get anywhere. He tried to imagine how it
might all have been, this very night even, if Mr. Helton
were still safe and sound out in his shack playing his
tune about feeling so good in the morning, drinking up
all the wine so you'd feel even better; and Mr. Hatch
safe in jail somewhere, mad as hops, maybe, but out of
harm's way and ready to listen to reason and to repent
of his meanness, the dirty, yellow-livered hound coming
around persecuting an innocent man and ruining a whole
family that never harmed him! Mr. Thompson felt the
veins of his forehead start up, his fists clutched as if they
seized an ax handle, the sweat broke out on him, he
bounded up from the bed with a yell smothered in his
throat, and Ellie started up after him, crying out, "Oh,
oh, don't! Don't! Don't!" as if she were having a nightmare. He stood shaking until his bones rattled in him,
crying hoarsely, "Light the lamp, light the lamp, Ellie."

Instead, Mrs. Thompson gave a shrill weak scream,
almost the same scream he had heard on that day she
came around the house when he was standing there with
the ax in his hand. He could not see her in the dark, but
she was on the bed, rolling violently. He felt for her in
horror, and his groping hands found her arms, up, and
her own hands pulling her hair straight out from her
head, her neck strained back, and the tight screams stran-

gling her. He shouted out for Arthur, for Herbert. "Your mother!" he bawled, his voice cracking. As he held Mrs. Thompson's arms, the boys came tumbling in, Arthur with the lamp above his head. By this light Mr. Thompson saw Mrs. Thompson's eyes, wide open, staring dreadfully at him, the tears pouring. She sat up at sight of the boys, and held out one arm towards them, the hand wagging in a crazy circle, then dropped on her back again, and suddenly went limp. Arthur set the lamp on the table and turned on Mr. Thompson. "She's scared," he said, "she's scared to death." His face was in a knot of rage, his fists were doubled up, he faced his father as if he meant to strike him. Mr. Thompson's jaw fell, he was so surprised he stepped back from the bed. Herbert went to the other side. They stood on each side of Mrs. Thompson and watched Mr. Thompson as if he were a dangerous wild beast. "What did you do to her?" shouted Arthur, in a grown man's voice. "You touch her again and I'll blow your heart out!" Herbert was pale and his cheek twitched, but he was on Arthur's side; he would do what he could to help Arthur.

Mr. Thompson had no fight left in him. His knees bent as he stood, his chest collapsed. "Why, Arthur," he said, his words crumbling and his breath coming short. "She's fainted again. Get the ammonia." Arthur did not move. Herbert brought the bottle, and handed it, shrinking, to his father.

Mr. Thompson held it under Mrs. Thompson's nose. He poured a little in the palm of his hand and rubbed it on her forehead. She gasped and opened her eyes and turned her head away from him. Herbert began a doleful hopeless sniffling. "Mamma," he kept saying, "Mamma, don't die."

"I'm all right," Mrs. Thompson said. "Now don't you worry around. Now Herbert, you mustn't do that. I'm all right." She closed her eyes. Mr. Thompson began pulling on his best pants; he put on his socks and shoes. The boys sat on each side of the bed, watching Mrs. Thompson's face. Mr. Thompson put on his shirt and coat. He said, "I reckon I'll ride over and get the doctor. Don't look like all this fainting is a good sign. Now you just keep watch until I get back." They listened, but said nothing. He said, "Don't you get any notions in your head. I never did your mother any harm in my life, on purpose." He went out, and, looking back, saw Herbert staring at him from under his brows, like a stranger. "You'll know how to look after her," said Mr. Thompson.

Mr. Thompson went through the kitchen. There he lighted the lantern, took a thin pad of scratch paper and a stub pencil from the shelf where the boys kept their schoolbooks. He swung the lantern on his arm and reached into the cupboard where he kept the guns. The shotgun was there to his hand, primed and ready, a man never knows when he may need a shotgun. He went out of the house without looking around, or looking back when he had left it, passed his barn without seeing it, and struck out to the farthest end of his fields, which ran for half a mile to the east. So many blows had been struck at Mr. Thompson and from so many directions he couldn't stop any more to find out where he was hit. He walked on, over plowed ground and over meadow, going through barbed wire fences cautiously, putting his gun through first; he could almost see in the dark, now his eyes were used to it. Finally he came to the last fence;

here he sat down, back against a post, lantern at his side, and, with the pad on his knee, moistened the stub pencil and began to write:

"Before Almighty God, the great judge of all before who I am about to appear, I do hereby solemnly swear that I did not take the life of Mr. Homer T. Hatch on purpose. It was done in defense of Mr. Helton. I did not aim to hit him with the ax but only to keep him off Mr. Helton. He aimed a blow at Mr. Helton who was not looking for it. It was my belief at the time that Mr. Hatch would of taken the life of Mr. Helton if I did not interfere. I have told all this to the judge and the jury and they let me off but nobody believes it. This is the only way I can prove I am not a cold blooded murderer like everybody seems to think. If I had been in Mr. Helton's place he would of done the same for me. I still think I done the only thing there was to do. My wife—"

Mr. Thompson stopped here to think a while. He wet the pencil point with the tip of his tongue and marked out the last two words. He sat a while blacking out the words until he had made a neat oblong patch where they had been, and started again:

"It was Mr. Homer T. Hatch who came to do wrong to a harmless man. He caused all this trouble and he deserved to die but I am sorry it was me who had to kill him."

He licked the point of his pencil again, and signed his full name carefully, folded the paper and put it in his outside pocket. Taking off his right shoe and sock, he set the butt of the shotgun along the ground with the twin barrels pointed towards his head. It was very awkward. He thought about this a little, leaning his head against the gun mouth. He was trembling and his head was drumming until he was deaf and blind, but he lay down flat on the earth on his side, drew the barrel under his chin and fumbled for the trigger with his great toe. That way he could work it.

PALE HORSE, PALE RIDER

In sleep she knew she was in her bed, but not the bed she had lain down in a few hours since, and the room was not the same but it was a room she had known somewhere. Her heart was a stone lying upon her breast outside of her; her pulses lagged and paused, and she knew that something strange was going to happen, even as the early morning winds were cool through the lattice, the streaks of light were dark blue and the whole house was snoring in its sleep.

Now I must get up and go while they are all quiet. Where are my things? Things have a will of their own in this place and hide where they like. Daylight will strike a sudden blow on the roof startling them all up to their feet; faces will beam asking, Where are you going, What are you doing, What are you thinking, How do you feel, Why do you say such things, What do you mean? No more sleep. Where are my boots and what horse shall I ride? Fiddler or Graylie or Miss Lucy with the long nose and the wicked eye? How I have loved this house in the morning before we are all awake and tangled together like badly cast fishing lines. Too many people have been born here, and have wept too much here, and have laughed too much, and have been too angry and out-rageous with each other here. Too many have died in this bed already, there are far too many ancestral bones propped up on the mantelpieces, there have been too damned many antimacassars in this house, she said loudly, and oh, what accumulation of storied dust never allowed to settle in peace for one moment.

And the stranger? Where is that lank greenish stranger I remember hanging about the place, welcomed by my grandfather, my great-aunt, my five times removed cousin, my decrepit hound and my silver kitten? Why did they take to him, I wonder? And where are they now? Yet I saw him pass the window in the evening. What else besides them did I have in the world? Nothing. Nothing is mine, I have only nothing but it is enough, it is beautiful and it is all mine. Do I even walk about in my own skin or is it something I have borrowed to spare my modesty? Now what horse shall I borrow for this journey I do not mean to take, Graylie or Miss Lucy or Fiddler who can jump ditches in the dark and knows how to get the bit between his teeth? Early morning is best for me because trees are trees in one stroke, stones are stones set in shades known to be grass, there are no false shapes or surmises, the road is still asleep with the crust of dew unbroken. I'll take Graylie because he is not afraid of bridges.

Come now, Graylie, she said, taking his bridle, we must outrun Death and the Devil. You are no good for it, she told the other horses standing saddled before the stable gate, among them the horse of the stranger, gray also, with tarnished nose and ears. The stranger swung into his saddle beside her, leaned far towards her and regarded her without meaning, the blank still stare of mindless malice that makes no threats and can bide its time. She drew Graylie around sharply, urged him to run. He leaped the low rose hedge and the narrow ditch beyond, and the dust of the lane flew heavily under his beating hoofs. The stranger rode beside her, easily, lightly, his reins loose in his half-closed hand, straight and elegant in dark shabby garments that flapped upon his bones; his pale face smiled in an evil trance, he did not glance at her. Ah, I have seen this fellow before, I know this man if I could place him. He is no stranger to me.

She pulled Graylie up, rose in her stirrups and shouted, I'm not going with you this time—ride on! Without pausing or turning his head the stranger rode on. Graylie's ribs heaved under her, her own ribs rose and fell, Oh, why am I so tired, I must wake up. "But let me get a fine yawn first," she said, opening her eyes and stretching, "a slap of cold water in my face, for I've been talking in my sleep again, I heard myself but what was I saying?"

Slowly, unwillingly, Miranda drew herself up inch by inch out of the pit of sleep, waited in a daze for life to begin again. A single word struck in her mind, a gong of warning, reminding her for the day long what she forgot happily in sleep, and only in sleep. The war, said the gong, and she shook her head. Dangling her feet idly with their slippers hanging, she was reminded of the way all sorts of persons sat upon her desk at the newspaper office. Every day she found someone there, sitting upon her desk instead of the chair provided, dangling his legs, eyes roving, full of his important affairs, waiting to pounce about something or other. "*Why* won't they sit in the chair? Should I put a sign on it, saying, 'For God's sake, sit here'?"

Far from putting up a sign, she did not even frown at her visitors. Usually she did not notice them at all until their determination to be seen was greater than her determination not to see them. Saturday, she thought, lying comfortably in her tub of hot water, will be pay day, as always. Or I hope always. Her thoughts roved hazily in a continual effort to bring together and unite firmly the disturbing oppositions in her day-to-day existence, where survival, she could see clearly, had become a series of feats of sleight of hand. I owe—let me see, I wish I had pencil and paper—well, suppose I *did* pay five dollars now on a Liberty Bond, I couldn't possibly keep it up. Or maybe. Eighteen dollars a week. So much for rent, so much for food, and I mean to have a few things besides. About five dollars' worth. Will leave me twenty-seven cents. I suppose I can make it. I suppose I should be worried. I am worried. Very well, now I am worried and what next? Twenty-seven cents. That's not so bad. Pure profit, really. Imagine if they should suddenly raise me to twenty I should then have two dollars and twenty-seven cents left over. But they aren't going to raise me to twenty. They are in fact going to throw me out if I don't buy a Liberty Bond. I hardly believe that. I'll ask Bill. (Bill was the city editor.) I wonder if a threat like that isn't a kind of blackmail. I don't believe even a Lusk Committeeman can get away with that.

Yesterday there had been two pairs of legs dangling, on either side of her typewriter, both pairs stuffed thickly into funnels of dark expensive-looking material. She noticed at a distance that one of them was oldish and one was youngish, and they both of them had a stale air of borrowed importance which apparently they had got from the same source. They were both much too well nourished and the younger one wore a square little mustache. Being what they were, no matter what their business was it would be something unpleasant. Miranda had nodded at them, pulled out her chair and without removing her cap or gloves had reached into a pile of letters and sheets from the copy desk as if she had not a moment to spare. They did not move, or take off their hats. At last she had said "Good morning" to them, and asked if they were, perhaps, waiting for her?

The two men slid off the desk, leaving some of her papers rumpled, and the oldish man had inquired why she had not bought a Liberty Bond. Miranda had looked at him then, and got a poor impression. He was a pursy-faced man, gross-mouthed, with little lightless eyes, and Miranda wondered why nearly all of those selected to do the war work at home were of his sort. He might be anything at all, she thought; advance agent for a road show, promoter of a wildcat oil company, a former saloon keeper announcing the opening of a new cabaret, an automobile salesman—any follower of any one of the crafty, haphazard callings. But he was now all Patriot, working for the government. "Look here," he asked her, "do you know there's a war, or don't you?"

Did he expect an answer to that? Be quiet, Miranda told herself, this was bound to happen. Sooner or later it happens. Keep your head. The man wagged his finger at her, "Do you?" he persisted, as if he were prompting an obstinate child.

"Oh, the war," Miranda had echoed on a rising note and she almost smiled at him. It was habitual, automatic, to give that solemn, mystically uplifted grin when you spoke the words or heard them spoken. "*C'est la guerre*," whether you could pronounce it or not, was even better, and always, always, you shrugged.

"Yeah," said the younger man in a nasty way, "the war." Miranda, startled by the tone, met his eye; his stare was really stony, really viciously cold, the kind of thing you might expect to meet behind a pistol on a deserted corner. This expression gave temporary meaning to a set of features otherwise nondescript, the face of those men who have no business of their own. "We're having a war, and some people are buying Liberty Bonds and others just don't seem to get around to it," he said. "That's what we mean."

Miranda frowned with nervousness, the sharp beginnings of fear. "Are you selling them?" she asked, taking the cover off her typewriter and putting it back again.

"No, we're not selling them," said the older man. "We're just asking you why you haven't bought one." The voice was persuasive and ominous.

Miranda began to explain that she had no money, and did not know where to find any, when the older man interrupted: "That's no excuse, no excuse at all, and you know it, with the Huns overrunning martyred Belgium."

"With our American boys fighting and dying in Belleau Wood," said the younger man, "anybody can raise fifty dollars to help beat the Boche."

Miranda said hastily, "I have eighteen dollars a week and not another cent in the world. I simply cannot buy anything."

"You can pay for it five dollars a week," said the older man (they had stood there cawing back and forth over her head), "like a lot of other people in this office, and a lot of other offices besides are doing."

Miranda, desperately silent, had thought, "Suppose I were not a coward, but said what I really thought? Suppose I said to hell with this filthy war? Suppose I asked that little thug, What's the matter with you, why aren't you rotting in Belleau Wood? I wish you were . . ."

She began to arrange her letters and notes, her fingers refusing to pick up things properly. The older man went on making his little set speech. It was hard, of course. Everybody was suffering, naturally. Everybody had to do his share. But as to that, a Liberty Bond was the safest investment you could make. It was just like having the money in the bank. Of course. The government was back of it and where better could you invest?

"I agree with you about that," said Miranda, "but I haven't any money to invest."

And of course, the man had gone on, it wasn't so much her fifty dollars that was going to make any difference. It was just a pledge of good faith on her part. A pledge of good faith that she was a loyal American doing her duty. And the thing was safe as a church. Why, if he had a million dollars he'd be glad to put every last cent of it in these Bonds. . . . "You can't lose by it," he said, almost benevolently, "and you can lose a lot if you don't. Think it over. You're the only one in this whole newspaper office that hasn't come in. And

every firm in this city has come in one hundred per cent.
Over at the *Daily Clarion* nobody had to be asked
twice."

"They pay better over there," said Miranda. "But next
week, if I can. Not now, next week."

"See that you do," said the younger man. "This ain't
any laughing matter."

They lolled away, past the Society Editor's desk, past
Bill the City Editor's desk, past the long copy desk where
old man Gibbons sat all night shouting at intervals,
"Jarge! Jarge!" and the copy boy would come flying.
"Never say *people* when you mean *persons*," old man
Gibbons had instructed Miranda, "and never say *practically*, say *virtually*, and don't for God's sake ever so
long as I am at this desk use the barbarism *inasmuch*
under any circumstances whatsoever. Now you're ed-
ucated, you may go." At the head of the stairs her in-
quisitors had stopped in their fussy pride and vainglory,
lighting cigars and wedging their hats more firmly over
their eyes.

Miranda turned over in the soothing water, and wished
she might fall asleep there, to wake up only when it was
time to sleep again. She had a burning slow headache,
and noticed it now, remembering she had waked up with
it and it had in fact begun the evening before. While she
dressed she tried to trace the insidious career of her
headache, and it seemed reasonable to suppose it had
started with the war. "It's been a headache, all right, but
not quite like this." After the Committeemen had left,
yesterday, she had gone to the cloakroom and had found
Mary Townsend, the Society Editor, quietly hysterical
about something. She was perched on the edge of the

shabby wicker couch with ridges down the center, knitting on something rose-colored. Now and then she would put down her knitting, seize her head with both hands and rock, saying, "My *God*," in a surprised, inquiring voice. Her column was called Ye Towne Gossyp, so of course everybody called her Towney. Miranda and Towney had a great deal in common, and liked each other. They had both been real reporters once, and had been sent together to "cover" a scandalous elopement, in which no marriage had taken place, after all, and the recaptured girl, her face swollen, had sat with her mother, who was moaning steadily under a mound of blankets. They had both wept painfully and implored the young reporters to suppress the worst of the story. They had suppressed it, and the rival newspaper printed it all the next day. Miranda and Towney had then taken their punishment together, and had been degraded publicly to routine female jobs, one to the theaters, the other to society. They had this in common, that neither of them could see what else they could possibly have done, and they knew they were considered fools by the rest of the staff—nice girls, but fools. At sight of Miranda, Towney had broken out in a rage, "I can't do it, I'll never be able to raise the money, I told them, I can't, I can't, but they wouldn't listen."

Miranda said, "I knew I wasn't the only person in this office who couldn't raise five dollars. I told them I couldn't, too, and I can't."

"My *God*," said Towney, in the same voice, "they told me I'd lose my job—"

"I'm going to ask Bill," Miranda said; "I don't believe Bill would do that."

"It's not up to Bill," said Towney. "He'd have to if

they got after him. Do you suppose they could put us in jail?"

"I don't know," said Miranda. "If they do, we won't be lonesome." She sat down beside Towney and held her own head. "What kind of soldier are you knitting that for? It's a sprightly color, it ought to cheer him up."

"Like hell," said Towney, her needles going again. "I'm making this for myself. That's that."

"Well," said Miranda, "we won't be lonesome and we'll catch up on our sleep." She washed her face and put on fresh make-up. Taking clean gray gloves out of her pocket she went out to join a group of young women fresh from the country club dances, the morning bridge, the charity bazaar, the Red Cross workrooms, who were wallowing in good works. They gave tea dances and raised money, and with the money they bought quantities of sweets, fruit, cigarettes, and magazines for the men in the cantonment hospitals. With this loot they were now setting out, a gay procession of high-powered cars and brightly tinted faces to cheer the brave boys who already, you might very well say, had fallen in defense of their country. It must be frightfully hard on them, the dears, to be floored like this when they're all crazy to get overseas and into the trenches as quickly as possible. Yes, and some of them are the cutest things you ever saw, I didn't know there were so many good-looking men in this country, good heavens, I said, where do they come from? Well, my dear, you may ask yourself that question, who knows where they did come from? You're quite right, the way I feel about it is this, we must do everything we can to make them contented, but I draw the line at talking to them. I told the chaperons at those dances for enlisted men, I'll dance with them, every dumbbell who asks me, but I will NOT talk to them, I said, even if there is a war. So I danced hundreds of miles without opening my mouth except to say, Please keep your knees to yourself. I'm glad we gave those dances up. Yes, and the men stopped coming, anyway. But listen, I've heard that a great many of the enlisted men come from very good families; I'm not good at catching names, and those I did catch I'd never heard before, so I don't know . . . but it seems to me if they were from good families, you'd know it, wouldn't you? I mean, if a man is well bred he doesn't step on your feet, does he? At least not that. I used to have a pair of sandals ruined at every one of those dances. Well, I think any kind of social life is in very poor taste just now, I think we should all put on our Red Cross head dresses and wear them for the duration of the war—

Miranda, carrying her basket and her flowers, moved in among the young women, who scattered out and rushed upon the ward uttering girlish laughter meant to be refreshingly gay, but there was a grim determined clang in it calculated to freeze the blood. Miserably embarrassed at the idiocy of her errand, she walked rapidly between the long rows of high beds, set foot to foot with a narrow aisle between. The men, a selected presentable lot, sheets drawn up to their chins, not seriously ill, were bored and restless, most of them willing to be amused at anything. They were for the most part picturesquely bandaged as to arm or head, and those who were not visibly wounded invariably replied "Rheumatism" if some tactless girl, who had been solemnly warned never to ask this question, still forgot and asked a man what his illness was. The good-natured, eager ones, laughing and calling out from their hard narrow beds, were soon surrounded. Miranda, with her wilting bouquet and her basket of sweets and cigarettes, looking about, caught the unfriendly bitter eye of a young fellow lying on his back, his right leg in a cast and pulley. She stopped at the foot of his bed and continued to look at him, and he looked back with an unchanged, hostile face. Not having any, thank you and be damned to the whole business, his eyes said plainly to her, and will you be so good as to take your trash off my bed? For Miranda had set it down, leaning over to place it where he might be able to reach it if he would. Having set it down, she was incapable of taking it up again, but hurried away, her face burning, down the long aisle and out into the cool October sunshine, where the dreary raw barracks swarmed and worked with an aimless life of scurrying, dun-colored insects; and going around to a window near where he lay, she looked in, spying upon her soldier. He was lying with his eyes closed, his eyebrows in a sad bitter frown. She could not place him at all, she could not imagine where he came from nor what sort of being he might have been "in life," she said to herself. His face was young and the features sharp and plain, the hands were not laborer's hands but not well-cared-for hands either. They were good useful properly shaped hands, lying there on the coverlet. It occurred to her that it would be her luck to find him, instead of a jolly hungry puppy glad of a bite to eat and a little chatter. It is like turning a corner absorbed in your painful thoughts and meeting your state of mind embodied, face to face, she said. "My own feelings about this whole thing, made flesh. Never again will I come here, this is no sort of thing to be doing.

This is disgusting," she told herself plainly. "Of course I would pick him out," she thought, getting into the back seat of the car she came in, "serves me right, I know better."

Another girl came out looking very tired and climbed in beside her. After a short silence, the girl said in a puzzled way, "I don't know what good it does, really. Some of them wouldn't take anything at all. I don't like this, do you?"

"I hate it," said Miranda.

"I suppose it's all right, though," said the girl, cautiously.

"Perhaps," said Miranda, turning cautious also.

That was for yesterday. At this point Miranda decided there was no good in thinking of yesterday, except for the hour after midnight she had spent dancing with Adam. He was in her mind so much, she hardly knew when she was thinking about him directly. His image was simply always present in more or less degree, he was sometimes nearer the surface of her thoughts, the pleasantest, the only really pleasant thought she had. She examined her face in the mirror between the windows and decided that her uneasiness was not all imagination. For three days at least she had felt odd and her expression was unfamiliar. She would have to raise that fifty dollars somehow, she supposed, or who knows what can happen? She was hardened to stories of personal disaster, of outrageous accusations and extraordinarily bitter penalties that had grown monstrously out of incidents very little more important than her failure—her refusal—to buy a Bond. No, she did not find herself a pleasing sight, flushed and shiny, and even her hair felt as if it had decided to grow in the other direction. I must do something about this, I can't let Adam see me like this, she told herself, knowing that even now at that moment he was listening for the turn of her door knob, and he would be in the hallway, or on the porch when she came out, as if by sheerest coincidence. The noon sunlight cast cold slanting shadows in the room where, she said, I suppose I live, and this day is beginning badly, but they all do now, for one reason or another. In a drowse, she sprayed perfume on her hair, put on her moleskin cap and jacket, now in their second winter, but still good, still nice to wear, again being glad she had paid a frightening price for them. She had enjoyed them all this time, and in no case would she have had the money now. Maybe she could manage for that Bond. She could not find the lock without leaning to search for it, then stood undecided a moment possessed by the notion that she had forgotten something she would miss seriously later on.

Adam was in the hallway, a step outside his own door; he swung about as if quite startled to see her, and said, "Hello. I don't have to go back to camp today after all—isn't that luck?"

Miranda smiled at him gaily because she was always delighted at the sight of him. He was wearing his new uniform, and he was all olive and tan and tawny, hay colored and sand colored from hair to boots. She half noticed again that he always began by smiling at her; that his smile faded gradually; that his eyes became fixed and thoughtful as if he were reading in a poor light.

They walked out together into the fine fall day, scuffling bright ragged leaves under their feet, turning their faces up to a generous sky really blue and spotless. At the first corner they waited for a funeral to pass, the mourners seated straight and firm as if proud in their sorrow.

"I imagine I'm late," said Miranda, "as usual. What time is it?"

"Nearly half past one," he said, slipping back his sleeve with an exaggerated thrust of his arm upward. The young soldiers were still self-conscious about their wrist watches. Such of them as Miranda knew were boys from southern and southwestern towns, far off the Atlantic seaboard, and they had always believed that only sissies wore wrist watches. "I'll slap you on the wrist watch," one vaudeville comedian would simper to another, and it was always a good joke, never stale.

"I think it's a most sensible way to carry a watch," said Miranda. "You needn't blush."

"I'm nearly used to it," said Adam, who was from Texas. "We've been told time and again how all the he-manly regular army men wear them. It's the horrors of war," he said; "are we downhearted? I'll say we are."

It was the kind of patter going the rounds. "You look it," said Miranda.

He was tall and heavily muscled in the shoulders, narrow in the waist and flanks, and he was infinitely buttoned, strapped, harnessed into a uniform as tough and unyielding in cut as a strait jacket, though the cloth was fine and supple. He had his uniforms made by the best tailor he could find, he confided to Miranda one day when she told him how squish he was looking in his new soldier suit. "Hard enough to make anything of the outfit, anyhow," he told her. "It's the least I can do for my beloved country, not to go around looking like a tramp." He was twenty-four years old and a Second

Lieutenant in an Engineers Corps, on leave because his outfit expected to be sent over shortly. "Came in to make my will," he told Miranda, "and get a supply of tooth-brushes and razor blades. By what gorgeous luck do you suppose," he asked her, "I happened to pick on your rooming house? How did I know you were there?"

Strolling, keeping step, his stout polished well-made boots setting themselves down firmly beside her thin-soled black suède, they put off as long as they could the end of their moment together, and kept up as well as they could their small talk that flew back and forth over little grooves worn in the thin upper surface of the brain, things you could say and hear clink reassuringly at once without disturbing the radiance which played and darted about the simple and lovely miracle of being two persons named Adam and Miranda, twenty-four years old each, alive and on the earth at the same moment: "Are you in the mood for dancing, Miranda?" and "I'm always in the mood for dancing, Adam!" but there were things in the way, the day that ended with dancing was a long way to go.

He really did look, Miranda thought, like a fine healthy apple this morning. One time or another in their talking, he had boasted that he had never had a pain in his life that he could remember. Instead of being hor-rified at this monster, she approved his monstrous uniqueness. As for herself, she had had too many pains to mention, so she did not mention them. After working for three years on a morning newspaper she had an il-lusion of maturity and experience; but it was fatigue merely, she decided, from keeping what she had been brought up to believe were unnatural hours, eating cas-ually at dirty little restaurants, drinking bad coffee all

night, and smoking too much. When she said something
of her way of living to Adam, he studied her face a few
seconds as if he had never seen it before, and said in a
forthright way, "Why, it hasn't hurt you a bit, I think
you're beautiful," and left her dangling there, wondering
if he had thought she wished to be praised. She did wish
to be praised, but not at that moment. Adam kept un-
wholesome hours too, or had in the ten days they had
known each other, staying awake until one o'clock to
take her out for supper; he smoked also continually,
though if she did not stop him he was apt to explain to
her exactly what smoking did to the lungs. "But," he
said, "does it matter so much if you're going to war,
anyway?"

"No," said Miranda, "and it matters even less if you're
staying at home knitting socks. Give me a cigarette, will
you?" They paused at another corner, under a half-
foliaged maple, and hardly glanced at a funeral procession approaching. His eyes were pale tan with orange
flecks in them, and his hair was the color of a haystack
when you turn the weathered top back to the clear straw
beneath. He fished out his cigarette case and snapped
his silver lighter at her, snapped it several times in his
own face, and they moved on, smoking.

"I can see you knitting socks," he said. "That would
be just your speed. You know perfectly well you can't
knit."

"I do worse," she said, soberly; "I write pieces ad-
vising other young women to knit and roll bandages and
do without sugar and help win the war."

"Oh, well," said Adam, with the easy masculine mor-
als in such questions, "that's merely your job, that
doesn't count."

"I wonder," said Miranda. "How did you manage to get an extension of leave?"

"They just gave it," said Adam, "for no reason. The men are dying like flies out there, anyway. This funny new disease. Simply knocks you into a cocked hat."

"It seems to be a plague," said Miranda, "something out of the Middle Ages. Did you ever see so many funerals, ever?"

"Never did. Well, let's be strong minded and not have any of it. I've got four days more straight from the blue and not a blade of grass must grow under our feet. What about tonight?"

"Same thing," she told him, "but make it about half past one. I've got a special job beside my usual run of the mill."

"What a job you've got," said Adam, "nothing to do but run from one dizzy amusement to another and then write a piece about it."

"Yes, it's too dizzy for words," said Miranda. They stood while a funeral passed, and this time they watched it in silence. Miranda pulled her cap to an angle and winked in the sunlight, her head swimming slowly "like goldfish," she told Adam, "my head swims. I'm only half awake, I must have some coffee."

They lounged on their elbows over the counter of a drug store. "No more cream for the stay-at-homes," she said, "and only one lump of sugar. I'll have two or none; that's the kind of martyr I'm being. I mean to live on boiled cabbage and wear shoddy from now on and get in good shape for the next round. No war is going to sneak up on me again."

"Oh, there won't be any more wars, don't you read the newspapers?" asked Adam. "We're going to mop 'em up this time, and they're going to stay mopped, and this is going to be all."

"So they told me," said Miranda, tasting her bitter lukewarm brew and making a rueful face. Their smiles approved of each other, they felt they had got the right tone, they were taking the war properly. Above all, thought Miranda, no tooth-gnashing, no hair-tearing, it's noisy and unbecoming and it doesn't get you anywhere.

"Swill," said Adam rudely, pushing back his cup. "Is that all you're having for breakfast?"

"It's more than I want," said Miranda.

"I had buckwheat cakes, with sausage and maple syrup, and two bananas, and two cups of coffee, at eight o'clock, and right now, again, I feel like a famished orphan left in the ashcan. I'm all set," said Adam, "for broiled steak and fried potatoes and—"

"Don't go on with it," said Miranda, "it sounds delirious to me. Do all that after I'm gone." She slipped from the high seat, leaned against it slightly, glanced at her face in her round mirror, rubbed rouge on her lips and decided that she was past praying for.

"There's something terribly wrong," she told Adam. "I feel too rotten. It can't just be the weather, and the war."

"The weather is perfect," said Adam, "and the war is simply too good to be true. But since when? You were all right yesterday."

"I don't know," she said slowly, her voice sounding small and thin. They stopped as always at the open door before the flight of littered steps leading up to the newspaper loft. Miranda listened for a moment to the rattle of typewriters above, the steady rumble of presses below.

"I wish we were going to spend the whole afternoon on a park bench," she said, "or drive to the mountains."

"I do too," he said; "let's do that tomorrow."

"Yes, tomorrow, unless something else happens. I'd like to run away," she told him; "let's both."

"Me?" said Adam. "Where I'm going there's no running to speak of. You mostly crawl about on your stomach here and there among the debris. You know, barbed wire and such stuff. It's going to be the kind of thing that happens once in a lifetime." He reflected a moment, and went on, "I don't know a darned thing about it, really, but they make it sound awfully messy. I've heard so much about it I feel as if I had been there and back. It's going to be an anticlimax," he said, "like seeing the pictures of a place so often you can't see it at all when you actually get there. Seems to me I've been in the army all my life."

Six months, he meant. Eternity. He looked so clear and fresh, and he had never had a pain in his life. She had seen them when they had been there and back and they never looked like this again. "Already the returned hero," she said, "and don't I wish you were."

"When I learned the use of the bayonet in my first training camp," said Adam, "I gouged the vitals out of more sandbags and sacks of hay than I could keep track of. They kept bawling at us, 'Get him, get that Boche, stick him before he sticks you'—and we'd go for those sandbags like wildfire, and honestly, sometimes I felt a perfect fool for getting so worked up when I saw the sand trickling out. I used to wake up in the night sometimes feeling silly about it."

"I can imagine," said Miranda. "It's perfect nonsense." They lingered, unwilling to say good-by. After a little pause, Adam, as if keeping up the conversation, asked, "Do you know what the average life expectation of a sapping party is after it hits the job?"

"Something speedy, I suppose."

"Just nine minutes," said Adam; "I read that in your own newspaper not a week ago."

"Make it ten and I'll come along," said Miranda.

"Not another second," said Adam, "exactly nine minutes, take it or leave it."

"Stop bragging," said Miranda. "Who figured that out?"

"A noncombatant," said Adam, "a fellow with rickets."

This seemed very comic, they laughed and leaned towards each other and Miranda heard herself being a little shrill. She wiped the tears from her eyes. "My, it's a funny war," she said; "isn't it? I laugh every time I think about it."

Adam took her hand in both of his and pulled a little at the tips of her gloves and sniffed them. "What nice perfume you have," he said, "and such a lot of it, too. I like a lot of perfume on gloves and hair," he said, sniffing again.

"I've got probably too much," she said. "I can't smell or see or hear today. I must have a fearful cold."

"Don't catch cold," said Adam; "my leave is nearly up and it will be the last, the very last." She moved her fingers in her gloves as he pulled at the fingers and turned her hands as if they were something new and curious and of great value, and she turned shy and quiet. She liked him, she liked him, and there was more than this but it was no good even imagining, because he was not for her nor for any woman, being beyond experience already, committed without any knowledge or act of his own to death. She took back her hands. "Good-by," she said finally, "until tonight."

She ran upstairs and looked back from the top. He was still watching her, and raised his hand without smiling. Miranda hardly ever saw anyone look back after he had said good-by. She could not help turning sometimes for one glimpse more of the person she had been talking with, as if that would save too rude and too sudden a snapping of even the lightest bond. But people hurried away, their faces already changed, fixed, in their straining towards their next stopping place, already absorbed in planning their next act or encounter. Adam was waiting as if he expected her to turn, and under his brows fixed in a strained frown, his eyes were very black.

At her desk she sat without taking off jacket or cap, slitting envelopes and pretending to read the letters. Only Chuck Rouncivale, the sports reporter, and Ye Towne Gossyp were sitting on her desk today, and them she liked having there. She sat on theirs when she pleased. Towney and Chuck were talking and they went on with it.

"They say," said Towney, "that it is really caused by germs brought by a German ship to Boston, a camouflaged ship, naturally, it didn't come in under its own colors. Isn't that ridiculous?"

"Maybe it was a submarine," said Chuck, "sneaking in from the bottom of the sea in the dead of night. Now that sounds better."

"Yes, it does," said Towney; "they always slip up somewhere in these details . . . and they think the germs were sprayed over the city—it started in Boston, you know—and somebody reported seeing a strange, thick, greasy-looking cloud float up out of Boston Harbor and spread slowly all over that end of town. I think it was an old woman who saw it."

"Should have been," said Chuck.

"I read it in a New York newspaper," said Towney; "so it's bound to be true."

Chuck and Miranda laughed so loudly at this that Bill stood up and glared at them. "Towney still reads the newspapers," explained Chuck.

"Well, what's funny about that?" asked Bill, sitting down again and frowning into the clutter before him.

"It was a noncombatant saw that cloud," said Miranda.

"Naturally," said Towney.

"Member of the Lusk Committee, maybe," said Miranda.

"The Angel of Mons," said Chuck, "or a dollar-a-year man."

Miranda wished to stop hearing, and talking, she wished to think for just five minutes of her own about Adam, really to think about him, but there was no time. She had seen him first ten days ago, and since then they had been crossing streets together, darting between trucks and limousines and pushcarts and farm wagons; he had waited for her in doorways and in little restaurants that smelled of stale frying fat; they had eaten and danced to the urgent whine and bray of jazz orchestras, they had sat in dull theaters because Miranda was there to write a piece about the play. Once they had gone to the mountains and, leaving the car, had climbed a stony trail, and had come out on a ledge upon a flat stone, where they sat and watched the lights change on a valley landscape that was, no doubt, Miranda said, quite apocryphal—"We need not believe it, but it is fine poetry," she told him; they had leaned their shoulders together there, and had sat quite still, watching. On two Sundays they had gone to the geological museum, and had pored in shared fascination over bits of meteors, rock formations, fossilized tusks and trees, Indian arrows, grottoes from the silver and gold lodes. "Think of those old miners washing out their fortunes in little pans beside the streams," said Adam, "and inside the earth there was this—" and he had told her he liked better those things that took long to make; he loved airplanes too, all sorts of machinery, things carved out of wood or stone. He knew nothing much about them, but he recognized them when he saw them. He had confessed that he simply could not get through a book, any kind of book except textbooks on engineering; reading bored him to crumbs; he regretted now he hadn't brought his roadster, but he hadn't thought he would need a car; he loved driving, he wouldn't expect her to believe how many hundreds of miles he could get over in a day . . . he had showed her snapshots of himself at the wheel of his roadster; of himself sailing a boat, looking very free and windblown, all angles, hauling on the ropes; he would have joined the air force, but his mother had hysterics every time he mentioned it. She didn't seem to realize that dog fighting in the air was a good deal safer than sapping parties on the ground at night. But he hadn't argued, because of course she did not realize about sapping parties. And here he was, stuck, on a plateau a mile high with no water for a boat and his car at home, otherwise they could really have had a good time. Miranda knew he was trying to tell her what kind of person he was when he had his machinery with him. She felt she knew pretty well what kind of person he was, and would have liked to tell him that if he thought he had left himself at home in a boat or an automobile, he was much mistaken. The telephones were ringing, Bill was shouting at somebody who kept saying, "Well, but listen, well, but listen—" but nobody was going to listen, of course, nobody. Old man Gibbons bellowed in despair, "Jarge, Jarge—"

"Just the same," Towney was saying in her most complacent patriotic voice. "Hut Service is a fine idea, and we should all volunteer even if they don't want us." Towney does well at this, thought Miranda, look at her; remembering the rose-colored sweater and the tight rebellious face in the cloakroom. Towney was now all open-faced glory and goodness, willing to sacrifice herself for her country. "After all," said Towney, "I *can* sing and dance well enough for the Little Theater, and I could write their letters for them, and at a pinch I might drive an ambulance. I have driven a Ford for years."

Miranda joined in: "Well, I can sing and dance too, but who's going to do the bed-making and the scrubbing up? Those huts are hard to keep, and it would be a dirty job and we'd be perfectly miserable; and as I've got a hard dirty job and am perfectly miserable, I'm going to stay at home."

"I think the women should keep out of it," said Chuck Rouncivale. "They just add skirts to the horrors of war." Chuck had bad lungs and fretted a good deal about missing the show. "I could have been there and back with a leg off by now; it would have served the old man right. Then he'd either have to buy his own hooch or sober up."

Miranda had seen Chuck on pay day giving the old man money for hooch. He was a good-humored ingratiating old scoundrel, too, that was the worst of him. He slapped his son on the back and beamed upon him with the bleared eye of paternal affection while he took his last nickel.

"It was Florence Nightingale ruined wars," Chuck went on. "What's the idea of petting soldiers and binding up their wounds and soothing their fevered brows? That's not war. Let 'em perish where they fall. That's what they're there for."

"You can talk," said Towney, with a slantwise glint at him.

"What's the idea?" asked Chuck, flushing and hunching his shoulders. "You know I've got this lung, or maybe half of it anyway by now."

"You're much too sensitive," said Towney. "I didn't mean a thing."

Bill had been raging about, chewing his half-smoked cigar, his hair standing up in a brush, his eyes soft and lambent but wild, like a stag's. He would never, thought Miranda, be more than fourteen years old if he lived for a century, which he would not, at the rate he was going. He behaved exactly like city editors in the moving pictures, even to the chewed cigar. Had he formed his style on the films, or had scenario writers seized once for all on the type Bill in its inarguable purity? Bill was shouting to Chuck: "*And* if he comes back here take him up the alley and saw his head off *by hand*!"

Chuck said, "He'll be back, don't worry." Bill said mildly, already off on another track, "Well, saw him off." Towney went to her own desk, but Chuck sat waiting amiably to be taken to the new vaudeville show. Miranda, with two tickets, always invited one of the reporters to go with her on Monday. Chuck was lavishly hardboiled and professional in his sports writing, but he had told Miranda that he didn't give a damn about sports, really; the job kept him out in the open, and paid him enough to buy the old man's hooch. He preferred shows and didn't see why women always had the job.

"Who does Bill want sawed today?" asked Miranda.

"That hoofer you panned in this morning's," said Chuck. "He was up here bright and early asking for the guy that writes up the show business. He said he was going to take the goof who wrote that piece up the alley and bop him in the nose. He said . . ."

"I hope he's gone," said Miranda; "I do hope he had to catch a train."

Chuck stood up and arranged his maroon-colored turtle-necked sweater, glanced down at the peasoup tweed plus fours and the hobnailed tan boots which he hoped would help to disguise the fact that he had a bad lung and didn't care for sports, and said, "He's long gone by now, don't worry. Let's get going; you're late as usual."

Miranda, facing about, almost stepped on the toes of a little drab man in a derby hat. He might have been a pretty fellow once, but now his mouth drooped where he had lost his side teeth, and his sad red-rimmed eyes had given up coquetry. A thin brown wave of hair was combed out with brilliantine and curled against the rim of the derby. He didn't move his feet, but stood planted with a kind of inert resistance, and asked Miranda: "Are you the so-called dramatic critic on this hick newspaper?"

"I'm afraid I am," said Miranda.

"Well," said the little man, "I'm just asking for one minute of your valuable time." His underlip shot out, he began with shaking hands to fish about in his waistcoat pocket. "I just hate to let you get away with it, that's all." He riffled through a collection of shabby newspaper clippings. "Just give these the once-over, will you? And then let me ask you if you think I'm gonna stand for being knocked by a tanktown critic," he said, in a toneless voice; "look here, here's Buffalo, Chicago, Saint Looey, Philadelphia, Frisco, besides New York. Here's the best publications in the business, *Variety*, the *Billboard*, they all broke down and admitted that Danny Dickerson knows his stuff. So you don't think so, hey? That's all I wanta ask you."

"No, I don't," said Miranda, as bluntly as she could, "and I can't stop to talk about it."

The little man leaned nearer, his voice shook as if he had been nervous for a long time. "Look here, what was there you didn't like about me? Tell me that."

Miranda said, "You shouldn't pay any attention at all. What does it matter what I think?"

"I don't care what you think, it ain't that," said the little man, "but these things get round and booking agencies back East don't know how it is out here. We get panned in the sticks and they think it's the same as getting panned in Chicago, see? They don't know the difference. They don't know that the more high class an act is the more the hick critics pan it. But I've been called the best

in the business by the best in the business and I wanta
know what you think is wrong with me."

Chuck said, "Come on, Miranda, curtain's going up."
Miranda handed the little man his clippings, they were
mostly ten years old, and tried to edge past him. He
stepped before her again and said without much conviction, "If you was a man I'd knock your block off."
Chuck got up at that and lounged over, taking his hands
out of his pockets, and said, "Now you've done your
song and dance you'd better get out. Get the hell out
now before I throw you downstairs."

The little man pulled at the top of his tie, a small blue
tie with red polka dots, slightly frayed at the knot. He
pulled it straight and repeated as if he had rehearsed it,
"Come out in the alley." The tears filled his thickened
red lids. Chuck said, "Ah, shut up," and followed Miranda, who was running towards the stairs. He overtook
her on the sidewalk. "I left him sniveling and shuffling
his publicity trying to find the joker," said Chuck, "the
poor old heel."

Miranda said, "There's too much of everything in this
world just now. I'd like to sit down here on the curb,
Chuck, and die, and never again see—I wish I could lose
my memory and forget my own name . . . I wish—"

Chuck said, "Toughen up, Miranda. This is no time
to cave in. Forget that fellow. For every hundred people
in show business, there are ninety-nine like him. But
you don't manage right, anyway. You bring it on yourself. All you have to do is play up the headliners, and
you needn't even mention the also-rans. Try to keep in
mind that Rypinsky has got show business cornered in
this town; please Rypinsky and you'll please the adver-

tising department, please them and you'll get a raise. Hand-in-glove, my poor dumb child, will you never learn?"

"I seem to keep learning all the wrong things," said Miranda, hopelessly.

"You do for a fact," Chuck told her cheerfully. "You are as good at it as I ever saw. Now do you feel better?"

"This is a rotten show you've invited me to," said Chuck. "Now what are you going to do about it? If I were writing it up, I'd—"

"Do write it up," said Miranda. "You write it up this time. I'm getting ready to leave, anyway, but don't tell anybody yet."

"You mean it? All my life," said Chuck, "I've yearned to be a so-called dramatic critic on a hick newspaper, and this is positively my first chance."

"Better take it," Miranda told him. "It may be your last." She thought, This is the beginning of the end of something. Something terrible is going to happen to me. I shan't need bread and butter where I'm going. I'll will it to Chuck, he has a venerable father to buy hooch for. I hope they let him have it. Oh, Adam, I hope I see you once more before I go under with whatever is the matter with me. "I wish the war were over," she said to Chuck, as if they had been talking about that. "I wish it were over and I wish it had never begun."

Chuck had got out his pad and pencil and was already writing his review. What she had said seemed safe enough but how would he take it? "I don't care how it started or when it ends," said Chuck, scribbling away, "I'm not going to be there."

All the rejected men talked like that, thought Miranda.

War was the one thing they wanted, now they couldn't have it. Maybe they had wanted badly to go, some of them. All of them had a sidelong eye for the women they talked with about it, a guarded resentment which said, "Don't pin a white feather on me, you bloodthirsty female. I've offered my meat to the crows and they won't have it." The worst thing about war for the stay-at-homes is there isn't anyone to talk to any more. The Lusk Committee will get you if you don't watch out. Bread will win the war. Work will win, sugar will win, peach pits will win the war. Nonsense. *Not* nonsense, I tell you, there's some kind of valuable high explosive to be got out of peach pits. So all the happy housewives hurry during the canning season to lay their baskets of peach pits on the altar of their country. It keeps them busy and makes them feel useful, and all these women running wild with the men away are dangerous, if they aren't given something to keep their little minds out of mischief. So rows of young girls, the intact cradles of the future, with their pure serious faces framed becomingly in Red Cross wimples, roll cock-eyed bandages that will never reach a base hospital, and knit sweaters that will never warm a manly chest, their minds dwelling lovingly on all the blood and mud and the next dance at the Acanthus Club for the officers of the flying corps. Keeping still and quiet will win the war.

"I'm simply not going to be there," said Chuck, absorbed in his review. No, Adam will be there, thought Miranda. She slipped down in the chair and leaned her head against the dusty plush, closed her eyes and faced for one instant that was a lifetime the certain, the overwhelming and awful knowledge that there was nothing at all ahead for Adam and for her. Nothing. She opened her eyes and held her hands together palms up, gazing at them and trying to understand oblivion.

"Now look at this," said Chuck, for the lights had come on and the audience was rustling and talking again. "I've got it all done, even before the headliner comes on. It's old Stella Mayhew, and she's always good, she's been good for forty years, and she's going to sing 'O the blues ain't nothin' but the easy-going heart disease.' That's all you need to know about her. Now just glance over this. Would you be willing to sign it?"

Miranda took the pages and stared at them conscientiously, turning them over, she hoped, at the right moment, and gave them back. "Yes, Chuck, yes, I'd sign that. But I won't. We must tell Bill you wrote it, because it's your start, maybe."

"You don't half appreciate it," said Chuck. "You read it too fast. Here, listen to this—" and he began to mutter excitedly. While he was reading she watched his face. It was a pleasant face with some kind of spark of life in it, and a good severity in the modeling of the brow above the nose. For the first time since she had known him she wondered what Chuck was thinking about. He looked preoccupied and unhappy, he wasn't so frivolous as he sounded. The people were crowding into the aisle, bringing out their cigarette cases ready to strike a match the instant they reached the lobby; women with waved hair clutched at their wraps, men stretched their chins to ease them of their stiff collars, and Chuck said, "We might as well go now." Miranda, buttoning her jacket, stepped into the moving crowd, thinking, What did I ever know about them? There must be a great many of them here who think as I do, and we dare not say a word to each other of our desperation, we are speechless animals letting ourselves be destroyed, and why? Does anybody here believe the things we say to each other?

Stretched in unease on the ridge of the wicker couch in the cloakroom, Miranda waited for time to pass and leave Adam with her. Time seemed to proceed with more than usual eccentricity, leaving twilight gaps in her mind for thirty minutes which seemed like a second, and then hard flashes of light that shone clearly on her watch proving that three minutes is an intolerable stretch of waiting, as if she were hanging by her thumbs. At last it was reasonable to imagine Adam stepping out of the house in the early darkness into the blue mist that might soon be rain, he would be on the way, and there was nothing to think about him, after all. There was only the wish to see him and the fear, the present threat, of not seeing him again; for every step they took towards each other seemed perilous, drawing them apart instead of together, as a swimmer in spite of his most determined strokes is yet drawn slowly backward by the tide. "I don't want to love," she would think in spite of herself, "not Adam, there is no time and we are not ready for it and yet this is all we have—"

And there he was on the sidewalk, with his foot on the first step, and Miranda almost ran down to meet him. Adam, holding her hands, asked, "Do you feel well now? Are you hungry? Are you tired? Will you feel like dancing after the show?"

"Yes to everything," said Miranda, "yes, yes. . . ." Her head was like a feather, and she steadied herself on his arm. The mist was still mist that might be rain later, and though the air was sharp and clean in her mouth, it did not, she decided, make breathing any easier. "I hope the show is good, or at least funny," she told him, "but I promise nothing."

It was a long, dreary play, but Adam and Miranda sat very quietly together waiting patiently for it to be over. Adam carefully and seriously pulled off her glove and held her hand as if he were accustomed to holding her hand in theaters. Once they turned and their eyes met, but only once, and the two pairs of eyes were equally steady and noncommittal. A deep tremor set up in Miranda, and she set about resisting herself methodically as if she were closing windows and doors and fastening down curtains against a rising storm. Adam sat watching the monotonous play with a strange shining excitement, his face quite fixed and still.

When the curtain rose for the third act, the third act did not take place at once. There was instead disclosed a backdrop almost covered with an American flag improperly and disrespectfully exposed, nailed at each upper corner, gathered in the middle and nailed again, sagging dustily. Before it posed a local dollar-a-year man, now doing his bit as a Liberty Bond salesman. He was an ordinary man past middle life, with a neat little melon buttoned into his trousers and waistcoat, an opinionated tight mouth, a face and figure in which nothing could be read save the inept sensual record of fifty years. But for once in his life he was an important fellow in an impressive situation, and he reveled, rolling his words in an actorish tone.

"Looks like a penguin," said Adam. They moved, smiled at each other, Miranda reclaimed her hand, Adam folded his together and they prepared to wear their way again through the same old moldy speech with the same old dusty backdrop. Miranda tried not to listen, but she heard. These vile Huns—glorious Belleau Wood—our keyword is Sacrifice—Martyred Belgium—give till it hurts—our noble boys Over There—Big Berthas—the death of civilization—the Boche—

"My head aches," whispered Miranda. "Oh, why won't he hush?"

"He won't," whispered Adam. "I'll get you some aspirin."

"In Flanders Field the poppies grow, Between the crosses row on row"—"He's getting into the home stretch," whispered Adam—atrocities, innocent babes hoisted on Boche bayonets—your child and my child—if our children are spared these things, then let us say with all reverence that these dead have not died in vain—the war, the *war*, the WAR to end WAR, war for Democracy for humanity, a safe world forever and ever—and to prove our faith in Democracy to each other, and to the world, let everybody get together and buy Liberty Bonds and do without sugar and wool socks—was that it? Miranda asked herself, Say that over, I didn't catch the last line. Did you mention Adam? If you didn't I'm not interested. What about Adam, you little pig? And what are we going to sing this time, "Tipperary" or "There's a Long, Long Trail"? Oh, please do let the show go on and get over with. I must write a piece about it before I can go dancing with Adam and we have no time. Coal, oil, iron, gold, international finance, why don't you tell us about them, you little liar?

The audience rose and sang, "There's a Long, Long Trail A-winding," their opened mouths black and faces pallid in the reflected footlights; some of the faces grimaced and wept and had shining streaks like snail's tracks on them. Adam and Miranda joined in at the tops of their voices, grinning shamefacedly at each other once or twice.

In the street, they lit their cigarettes and walked slowly as always. "Just another nasty old man who would like to see the young ones killed," said Miranda in a low voice; "the tomcats try to eat the little tomkittens, you know. They don't fool you really, do they, Adam?"

The young people were talking like that about the business by then. They felt they were seeing pretty clearly through that game. She went on, "I hate these potbellied baldheads, too fat, too old, too cowardly, to go to war themselves, they know they're safe; it's you they are sending instead—"

Adam turned eyes of genuine surprise upon her. "Oh, *that* one," he said. "Now what could the poor sap do if they did take him? It's not his fault," he explained, "he can't do anything but talk." His pride in his youth, his forbearance and tolerance and contempt for that unlucky being breathed out of his very pores as he strolled, straight and relaxed in his strength. "What *could* you expect of him, Miranda?"

She spoke his name often, and he spoke hers rarely. The little shock of pleasure the sound of her name in his mouth gave her stopped her answer. For a moment she hesitated, and began at another point of attack "Adam," she said, "the worst of war is the fear and suspicion and the awful expression in all the eyes you meet . . . as if they had pulled down the shutters over their minds and their hearts and were peering out at you, ready to leap if you make one gesture or say one word they do not understand instantly. It frightens me; I live in fear too, and no one should have to live in fear. It's the skulking about, and the lying. It's what war does to the mind and

the heart, Adam, and you can't separate these two—
what it does to them is worse than what it can do to the
body."

Adam said soberly, after a moment, "Oh, yes, but
suppose one comes back whole? The mind and the heart
sometimes get another chance, but if anything happens
to the poor old human frame, why, it's just out of luck,
that's all."

"Oh, yes," mimicked Miranda. "It's just out of luck,
that's all."

"If I didn't go," said Adam, in a matter-of-fact voice,
"I couldn't look myself in the face."

So that's all settled. With her fingers flattened on his
arm, Miranda was silent, thinking about Adam. No,
there was no resentment or revolt in him. Pure, she
thought, all the way through, flawless, complete, as the
sacrificial lamb must be. The sacrificial lamb strode along
casually, accommodating his long pace to hers, keeping
her on the inside of the walk in the good American style,
helping her across street corners as if she were a
cripple—"I hope we don't come to a mud puddle, he'll
carry me over it"—giving off whiffs of tobacco smoke,
a manly smell of scentless soap, freshly cleaned leather
and freshly washed skin, breathing through his nose and
carrying his chest easily. He threw back his head and
smiled into the sky which still misted, promising rain.
"Oh, boy," he said, "what a night. Can't you hurry
that review of yours so we can get started?"

He waited for her before a cup of coffee in the restaurant next to the pressroom, nicknamed The Greasy
Spoon. When she came down at last, freshly washed and
combed and powdered, she saw Adam first, sitting near
the dingy big window, face turned to the street, but

looking down. It was an extraordinary face, smooth and
fine and golden in the shabby light, but now set in a
blind melancholy, a look of pained suspense and disil-
lusion. For just one split second she got a glimpse of
Adam when he would have been older, the face of the
man he would not live to be. He saw her then, rose, and
the bright glow was there.

Adam pulled their chairs together at their table; they
drank hot tea and listened to the orchestra jazzing "Pack
Up Your Troubles."

"In an old kit bag, and smoil, smoil, smoil," shouted
half a dozen boys under the draft age, gathered around
a table near the orchestra. They yelled incoherently,
laughed in great hysterical bursts of something that appeared to be merriment, and passed around under the
tablecloth flat bottles containing a clear liquid—for in
this western city founded and built by roaring drunken
miners, no one was allowed to take his alcohol openly
—splashed it into their tumblers of ginger ale, and went
on singing, "It's a Long Way to Tipperary." When the
tune changed to "Madelon," Adam said, "Let's dance."
It was a tawdry little place, crowded and hot and full of
smoke, but there was nothing better. The music was
gay; and life is completely crazy anyway, thought Miranda, so what does it matter? This is what we have,
Adam and I, this is all we're going to get, this is the way
it is with us. She wanted to say, "Adam, come out of
your dream and listen to me. I have pains in my chest
and my head and my heart and they're real. I am in pain
all over, and you are in such danger as I can't bear to
think about, and why can we not save each other?" When
her hand tightened on his shoulder his arm tightened

about her waist instantly, and stayed there, holding firmly. They said nothing but smiled continually at each other, odd changing smiles as though they had found a new language. Miranda, her face near Adam's shoulder, noticed a dark young pair sitting at a corner table, each with an arm around the waist of the other, their heads together, their eyes staring at the same thing, whatever it was, that hovered in space before them. Her right hand lay on the table, his hand over it, and her face was a blur with weeping. Now and then he raised her hand and kissed it, and set it down and held it, and her eyes would fill again. They were not shameless, they had merely forgotten where they were, or they had no other place to go, perhaps. They said not a word, and the small pantomime repeated itself, like a melancholy short film running monotonously over and over again. Miranda envied them. She envied that girl. At least she can weep if that helps, and he does not even have to ask, What is the matter? Tell me. They had cups of coffee before them, and after a long while—Miranda and Adam had danced and sat down again twice—when the coffee was quite cold, they drank it suddenly, then embraced as before, without a word and scarcely a glance at each other. Something was done and settled between them, at least; it was enviable, enviable, that they could sit quietly together and have the same expression on their faces while they looked into the hell they shared, no matter what kind of hell, it was theirs, they were together.

At the table nearest Adam and Miranda a young woman was leaning on her elbow, telling her young man a story. "And I don't like him because he's too fresh. He kept on asking me to take a drink and I kept telling him, I don't drink and he said, Now look here, I want a drink the worst way and I think it's mean of you not to drink with me, I can't sit up here and drink by myself, he said. I told him, You're not by yourself in the first place; I like that, I said, and if you want a drink go ahead and have it, I told him, why drag *me* in? So he called the waiter and ordered ginger ale and two glasses and I drank straight ginger ale like I always do but he poured a shot of hooch in his. He was awfully proud of that hooch, said he made it himself out of potatoes. Nice homemade likker, warm from the pipe, he told me, three drops of this and your ginger ale will taste like Mumm's Extry. But I said, No, and I mean no, can't you get that through your bean? He took another drink and said, Ah, come on, honey, don't be so stubborn, this'll make your shimmy shake. So I just got tired of the argument, and I said, I don't need to drink, to shake my shimmy, I can strut my stuff on tea, I said. Well, why don't you then, he wanted to know, and I just told him—"

She knew she had been asleep for a long time when all at once without even a warning footstep or creak of the door hinge, Adam was in the room turning on the light, and she knew it was he, though at first she was blinded and turned her head away. He came over at once and sat on the side of the bed and began to talk as if he were going on with something they had been talking about before. He crumpled a square of paper and tossed it in the fireplace.

"You didn't get my note," he said. "I left it under the door. I was called back suddenly to camp for a lot of inoculations. They kept me longer than I expected, I was late. I called the office and they told me you were not coming in today. I called Miss Hobbe here and she said you were in bed and couldn't come to the telephone. Did she give you my message?"

"No," said Miranda drowsily, "but I think I have been asleep all day. Oh, I do remember. There was a doctor here. Bill sent him. I was at the telephone once, for Bill told me he would send an ambulance and have me taken to the hospital. The doctor tapped my chest and left a prescription and said he would be back, but he hasn't come."

"Where is it, the prescription?" asked Adam.

"I don't know. He left it, though, I saw him."

Adam moved about searching the tables and the mantelpiece. "Here it is," he said. "I'll be back in a few minutes. I must look for an all-night drug store. It's after one o'clock. Good-by."

Good-by, good-by. Miranda watched the door where he had disappeared for quite a while, then closed her eyes, and thought, When I am not here I cannot remember anything about this room where I have lived for nearly a year, except that the curtains are too thin and there was never any way of shutting out the morning light. Miss Hobbe had promised heavier curtains, but they had never appeared. When Miranda in her dressing gown had been at the telephone that morning, Miss Hobbe had passed through, carrying a tray. She was a little red-haired nervously friendly creature, and her manner said all too plainly that the place was not paying and she was on the ragged edge.

"My dear *child*," she said sharply, with a glance at Miranda's attire, "what is the matter?"

Miranda, with the receiver to her ear, said, "Influenza, I think."

"*Horrors*," said Miss Hobbe, in a whisper, and the tray wavered in her hands. "Go back to bed at once . . . go at *once*!"

"I must talk to Bill first," Miranda had told her, and Miss Hobbe had hurried on and had not returned. Bill had shouted directions at her, promising everything, doctor, nurse, ambulance, hospital, her check every week as usual, everything, but she was to get back to bed and stay there. She dropped into bed, thinking that Bill was the only person she had ever seen who actually tore his own hair when he was excited enough . . . I suppose I should ask to be sent home, she thought, it's a respectable old custom to inflict your death on the family if you can manage it. No, I'll stay here, this is my business, but not in this room, I hope . . . I wish I were in the cold mountains in the snow, that's what I should like best; and all about her rose the measured ranges of the Rockies wearing their perpetual snow, their majestic blue laurels of cloud, chilling her to the bone with their sharp breath. Oh, no, I must have warmth— and her memory turned and roved after another place she had known first and loved best, that now she could see only in drifting fragments of palm and cedar, dark shadows and a sky that warmed without dazzling, as this strange sky had dazzled without warming her; there was the long slow wavering of gray moss in the drowsy oak shade, the spacious hovering of buzzards overhead, the smell of crushed water herbs along a bank, and without warning a broad tranquil river into which flowed all the rivers she had known. The walls shelved away in one deliberate silent movement on either side, and a tall sailing ship was moored near by, with a gangplank weath-

ered to blackness touching the foot of her bed. Back of
the ship was jungle, and even as it appeared before her,
she knew it was all she had ever read or had been told
or felt or thought about jungles; a writhing terribly alive
and secret place of death, creeping with tangles of spotted
serpents, rainbow-colored birds with malign eyes, leop-
ards with humanly wise faces and extravagantly crested
lions; screaming long-armed monkeys tumbling among
broad fleshy leaves that glowed with sulphur-colored
light and exuded the ichor of death, and rotting trunks
of unfamiliar trees sprawled in crawling slime. Without
surprise, watching from her pillow, she saw herself run
swiftly down this gangplank to the slanting deck, and
standing there, she leaned on the rail and waved gaily to
herself in bed, and the slender ship spread its wings and
sailed away into the jungle. The air trembled with the
shattering scream and the hoarse bellow of voices all
crying together, rolling and colliding above her like ragged stormclouds, and the words became two words only
rising and falling and clamoring about her head. Danger,
danger, danger, the voices said, and War, war, war.
There was her door half open, Adam standing with his
hand on the knob, and Miss Hobbe with her face all out
of shape with terror was crying shrilly, "I tell you, they
must come for her *now*, or I'll put her on the sidewalk
. . . I tell you, this is a plague, a plague, my God, and
I've got a houseful of people to think about!"

Adam said, "I know that. They'll come for her tomorrow morning."

"Tomorrow morning, my God, they'd better come
now!"

"They can't get an ambulance," said Adam, "and there

aren't any beds. And we can't find a doctor or a nurse. They're all busy. That's all there is to it. You stay out of the room, and I'll look after her."

"Yes, you'll look after her, I can see that," said Miss Hobbe, in a particularly unpleasant tone.

"Yes, that's what I said," answered Adam, drily, "and you keep out."

He closed the door carefully. He was carrying an assortment of misshapen packages, and his face was astonishingly impassive.

"Did you hear that?" he asked, leaning over and speaking very quietly.

"Most of it," said Miranda, "it's a nice prospect, isn't it?"

"I've got your medicine," said Adam, "and you're to begin with it this minute. She can't put you out."

"So it's really as bad as that," said Miranda.

"It's as bad as anything can be," said Adam, "all the theaters and nearly all the shops and restaurants are closed, and the streets have been full of funerals all day and ambulances all night—"

"But not one for me," said Miranda, feeling hilarious and lightheaded. She sat up and beat her pillow into shape and reached for her robe. "I'm glad you're here, I've been having a nightmare. Give me a cigarette, will you, and light one for yourself and open all the windows and sit near one of them. You're running a risk," she told him, "don't you know that? Why do you do it?"

"Never mind," said Adam, "take your medicine," and offered her two large cherry-colored pills. She swallowed them promptly and instantly vomited them up. "*Do* excuse me," she said, beginning to laugh. "I'm so sorry."

Adam without a word and with a very concerned expression washed her face with a wet towel, gave her some cracked ice from one of the packages, and firmly offered her two more pills. "That's what they always did at home," she explained to him, "and it worked." Crushed with humiliation, she put her hands over her face and laughed again, painfully.

"There are two more kinds yet," said Adam, pulling her hands from her face and lifting her chin. "You've hardly begun. And I've got other things, like orange juice and ice cream—they told me to feed you ice cream—and coffee in a thermos bottle, and a thermometer. You have to work through the whole lot so you'd better take it easy."

"This time last night we were dancing," said Miranda, and drank something from a spoon. Her eyes followed him about the room, as he did things for her with an absent-minded face, like a man alone; now and again he would come back, and slipping his hand under her head, would hold a cup or a tumbler to her mouth, and she drank, and followed him with her eyes again, without a clear notion of what was happening.

"Adam," she said, "I've just thought of something. Maybe they forgot St. Luke's Hospital. Call the sisters there and ask them not to be so selfish with their silly old rooms. Tell them I only want a very small dark ugly one for three days, or less. Do try them, Adam."

He believed, apparently, that she was still more or less in her right mind, for she heard him at the telephone explaining in his deliberate voice. He was back again almost at once, saying, "This seems to be my day for getting mixed up with peevish old maids. The sister said that even if they had a room you couldn't have it without doctor's orders. But they didn't have one, anyway. She was pretty sour about it."

"Well," said Miranda in a thick voice, "I think that's abominably rude and mean, don't you?" She sat up with a wide gesture of both arms, and began to retch again, violently.

"Hold it, as you were," called Adam, fetching the basin. He held her head, washed her face and hands with ice water, put her head straight on the pillow, and went over and looked out of the window. "Well," he said at last, sitting beside her again, "they haven't got a room. They haven't got a bed. They haven't even got a baby crib, the way she talked. So I think that's straight enough, and we may as well dig in."

"Isn't the ambulance coming?"

"Tomorrow, maybe."

He took off his tunic and hung it on the back of a chair. Kneeling before the fireplace, he began carefully to set kindling sticks in the shape of an Indian tepee, with a little paper in the center for them to lean upon. He lighted this and placed other sticks upon them, and larger bits of wood. When they were going nicely he added still heavier wood, and coal a few lumps at a time, until there was a good blaze, and a fire that would not need rekindling. He rose and dusted his hands together, the fire illuminated him from the back and his hair shone.

"Adam," said Miranda, "I think you're very beautiful." He laughed out at this, and shook his head at her. "What a hell of a word," he said, "for me." "It was the first that occurred to me," she said, drawing up on her elbow to catch the warmth of the blaze. "That's a good job, that fire."

He sat on the bed again, dragging up a chair and putting his feet on the rungs. They smiled at each other for the first time since he had come in that night. "How do you feel now?" he asked.

"Better, much better," she told him. "Let's talk. Let's tell each other what we meant to do."

"You tell me first," said Adam. "I want to know about you."

"You'd get the notion I had a very sad life," she said, "and perhaps it was, but I'd be glad enough to have it now. If I could have it back, it would be easy to be happy about almost anything at all. That's not true, but that's the way I feel now." After a pause, she said, "There's nothing to tell, after all, if it ends now, for all this time I was getting ready for something that was going to happen later, when the time came. So now it's nothing much."

"But it must have been worth having until now, wasn't it?" he asked seriously as if it were something important to know.

"Not if this is all," she repeated obstinately.

"Weren't you ever—happy?" asked Adam, and he was plainly afraid of the word; he was shy of it as he was of the word *love*, he seemed never to have spoken it before, and was uncertain of its sound or meaning.

"I don't know," she said, "I just lived and never thought about it. I remember things I liked, though, and things I hoped for."

"I was going to be an electrical engineer," said Adam. He stopped short. "And I shall finish up when I get back," he added, after a moment.

"Don't you love being alive?" asked Miranda. "Don't you love weather and the colors at different times of the

day, and all the sounds and noises like children screaming
in the next lot, and automobile horns and little bands
playing in the street and the smell of food cooking?"

"I love to swim, too," said Adam.

"So do I," said Miranda; "we never did swim together."

"Do you remember any prayers?" she asked him suddenly. "Did you ever learn anything at Sunday School?"

"Not much," confessed Adam without contrition.
"Well, the Lord's Prayer."

"Yes, and there's Hail Mary," she said, "and the really
useful one beginning, I confess to Almighty God and to
blessed Mary ever virgin and to the holy Apostles Peter
and Paul—"

"Catholic," he commented.

"Prayers just the same, you big Methodist. I'll bet you
are a Methodist."

"No, Presbyterian."

"Well, what others do you remember?"

"Now I lay me down to sleep—" said Adam.

"Yes, that one, and Blessed Jesus meek and mild—
you see that my religious education wasn't neglected
either. I even know a prayer beginning O Apollo. Want
to hear it?"

"No," said Adam, "you're making fun."

"I'm not," said Miranda, "I'm trying to keep from
going to sleep. I'm afraid to go to sleep, I may not wake
up. Don't let me go to sleep, Adam. Do you know
Matthew, Mark, Luke and John? Bless the bed I lie
upon?"

"If I should die before I wake, I pray the Lord my
soul to take. Is that it?" asked Adam. "It doesn't sound
right, somehow."

"Light me a cigarette, please, and move over and sit near the window. We keep forgetting about fresh air. You must have it." He lighted the cigarette and held it to her lips. She took it between her fingers and dropped it under the edge of her pillow. He found it and crushed it out in the saucer under the water tumbler. Her head swam in darkness for an instant, cleared, and she sat up in panic, throwing off the covers and breaking into a sweat. Adam leaped up with an alarmed face, and almost at once was holding a cup of hot coffee to her mouth.

"You must have some too," she told him, quiet again, and they sat huddled together on the edge of the bed, drinking coffee in silence.

Adam said, "You must lie down again. You're awake now."

"Let's sing," said Miranda. "I know an old spiritual, I can remember some of the words." She spoke in a natural voice. "I'm fine now." She began in a hoarse whisper, " 'Pale horse, pale rider, done taken my lover away . . .' Do you know that song?"

"Yes," said Adam, "I heard Negroes in Texas sing it, in an oil field."

"I heard them sing it in a cotton field," she said; "it's a good song."

They sang that line together. "But I can't remember what comes next," said Adam.

" 'Pale horse, pale rider,' " said Miranda, "(We really need a good banjo) 'done taken my lover away—' " Her voice cleared and she said, "But we ought to get on with it. What's the next line?"

"There's a lot more to it than that," said Adam, "about forty verses, the rider done taken away mammy, pappy, brother, sister, the whole family besides the lover—"

"But not the singer, not yet," said Miranda. "Death always leaves one singer to mourn. 'Death,' " she sang, " 'oh, leave one singer to mourn—' "

" 'Pale horse, pale rider,' " chanted Adam, coming in on the beat, " 'done taken my lover away!' (I think we're good, I think we ought to get up an act—)"

"Go in Hut Service," said Miranda, "entertain the poor defenseless heroes Over There."

"We'll play banjos," said Adam; "I always wanted to play the banjo."

Miranda sighed, and lay back on the pillow and thought, I must give up, I can't hold out any longer. There was only that pain, only that room, and only Adam. There were no longer any multiple planes of living, no tough filaments of memory and hope pulling taut backwards and forwards holding her upright between them. There was only this one moment and it was a dream of time, and Adam's face, very near hers, eyes still and intent, was a shadow, and there was to be nothing more. . . .

"Adam," she said out of the heavy soft darkness that drew her down, down, "I love you, and I was hoping you would say that to me, too."

He lay down beside her with his arm under her shoulder, and pressed his smooth face against hers, his mouth moved towards her mouth and stopped. "Can you hear what I am saying? . . . What do you think I have been trying to tell you all this time?"

She turned towards him, the cloud cleared and she saw his face for an instant. He pulled the covers about her and held her, and said, "Go to sleep, darling, darling, if you will go to sleep now for one hour I will wake you up and bring you hot coffee and tomorrow we will find somebody to help. I love you, go to sleep—"

Almost with no warning at all, she floated into the darkness, holding his hand, in sleep that was not sleep but clear evening light in a small green wood, and angry dangerous wood full of inhuman concealed voices singing sharply like the whine of arrows and she saw Adam transfixed by a flight of these singing arrows that struck him in the heart and passed shrilly cutting their path through the leaves. Adam fell straight back before her eyes, and rose again unwounded and alive; another flight of arrows loosed from the invisible bow struck him again and he fell, and yet he was there before her untouched in a perpetual death and resurrection. She threw herself before him, angrily and selfishly she interposed between him and the track of the arrow, crying, No, no, like a child cheated in a game, It's my turn now, why must you always be the one to die? and the arrows struck her cleanly through the heart and through his body and he lay dead, and she still lived, and the wood whistled and sang and shouted, every branch and leaf and blade of grass had its own terrible accusing voice. She ran then, and Adam caught her in the middle of the room, running, and said, "Darling, I must have been asleep too. What happened, you screamed terribly?"

After he had helped her to settle again, she sat with her knees drawn up under her chin, resting her head on her folded arms and began carefully searching for her words because it was important to explain clearly. "It was a very odd sort of dream, I don't know why it could have frightened me. There was something about an old-fashioned valentine. There were two hearts carved on a tree, pierced by the same arrow—you know, Adam—"

"Yes, I know, honey," he said in the gentlest sort of way, and sat kissing her on the cheek and forehead with a kind of accustomedness, as if he had been kissing her for years, "one of those lace paper things."

"Yes, and yet they were alive, and were us, you understand—this doesn't seem to be quite the way it was, but it was something like that. It was in a wood—"

"Yes," said Adam. He got up and put on his tunic and gathered up the thermos bottle. "I'm going back to that little stand and get us some ice cream and hot coffee," he told her, "and I'll be back in five minutes, and you keep quiet. Good-by for five minutes," he said, holding her chin in the palm of his hand and trying to catch her eye, "and you be very quiet."

"Good-by," she said. "I'm awake again." But she was not, and the two alert young internes from the County hospital who had arrived, after frantic urgings from the noisy city editor of the Blue Mountain *News*, to carry her away in a police ambulance, decided that they had better go down and get the stretcher. Their voices roused her, she sat up, got out of bed at once and stood glancing about brightly. "Why, you're all right," said the darker and stouter of the two young men, both extremely fit and competent-looking in their white clothes, each with a flower in his buttonhole. "I'll just carry you." He unfolded a white blanket and wrapped it around her. She gathered up the folds and asked, "But where is Adam?" taking hold of the doctor's arm. He laid a hand on her drenched forehead, shook his head, and gave her a shrewd look. "Adam?"

"Yes," Miranda told him, lowering her voice confidentially, "he was here and now he is gone."

"Oh, he'll be back," the interne told her easily, "he's just gone round the block to get cigarettes. Don't worry about Adam. He's the least of your troubles."

"Will he know where to find me?" she asked, still holding back.

"We'll leave him a note," said the interne. "Come now, it's time we got out of here."

He lifted and swung her up to his shoulder. "I feel very badly," she told him; "I don't know why."

"I'll bet you do," said he, stepping out carefully, the other doctor going before them, and feeling for the first step of the stairs. "Put your arms around my neck," he instructed her. "It won't do you any harm and it's a great help to me."

"What's your name?" Miranda asked as the other doctor opened the front door and they stepped out into the frosty sweet air.

"Hildesheim," he said, in the tone of one humoring a child.

"Well, Dr. Hildesheim, aren't we in a pretty mess?"

"We certainly are," said Dr. Hildesheim.

The second young interne, still quite fresh and dapper in his white coat, though his carnation was withering at the edges, was leaning over listening to her breathing through a stethoscope, whistling thinly, "There's a Long, Long Trail—" From time to time he tapped her ribs smartly with two fingers, whistling. Miranda observed him for a few moments until she fixed his bright busy hazel eye not four inches from hers. "I'm not un-

conscious," she explained, "I know what I want to say."
Then to her horror she heard herself babbling nonsense,
knowing it was nonsense though she could not hear what
she was saying. The flicker of attention in the eye near
her vanished, the second interne went on tapping and
listening, hissing softly under his breath.

"I wish you'd stop whistling," she said clearly. The
sound stopped. "It's a beastly tune," she added. Anything, anything at all to keep her small hold on the life
of human beings, a clear line of communication, no matter what, between her and the receding world. "Please
let me see Dr. Hildesheim," she said, "I have something
important to say to him. I must say it now." The second
interne vanished. He did not walk away, he fled into the
air without a sound, and Dr. Hildesheim's face appeared
in his stead.

"Dr. Hildesheim, I want to ask you about Adam."

"That young man? He's been here, and left you a note,
and has gone again," said Dr. Hildesheim, "and he'll be
back tomorrow and the day after." His tone was altogether too merry and flippant.

"I don't believe you," said Miranda, bitterly, closing
her lips and eyes and hoping she might not weep.

"Miss Tanner," called the doctor, "have you got that
note?"

Miss Tanner appeared beside her, handed her an un-
sealed envelope, took it back, unfolded the note and gave
it to her.

"I can't see it," said Miranda, after a pained search of
the page full of hasty scratches in black ink.

"Here, I'll read it," said Miss Tanner. "It says, 'They
came and took you while I was away and now they will
not let me see you. Maybe tomorrow they will, with

my love, Adam,' " read Miss Tanner in a firm dry voice, pronouncing the words distinctly. "Now, do you see?" she asked soothingly.

Miranda, hearing the words one by one, forgot them one by one. "Oh, read it again, what does it say?" she called out over the silence that pressed upon her, reaching towards the dancing words that just escaped as she almost touched them. "That will do," said Dr. Hildesheim, calmly authoritarian. "Where is that bed?"

"There is no bed yet," said Miss Tanner, as if she said, We are short of oranges. Dr. Hildesheim said, "Well, we'll manage something," and Miss Tanner drew the narrow trestle with bright crossed metal supports and small rubbery wheels into a deep jut of the corridor, out of the way of the swift white figures darting about, whirling and skimming like water flies all in silence. The white walls rose sheer as cliffs, a dozen frosted moons followed each other in perfect self-possession down a white lane and dropped mutely one by one into a snowy abyss.

What is this whiteness and silence but the absence of pain? Miranda lay lifting the nap of her white blanket softly between eased fingers, watching a dance of tall deliberate shadows moving behind a wide screen of sheets spread upon a frame. It was there, near her, on her side of the wall where she could see it clearly and enjoy it, and it was so beautiful she had no curiosity as to its meaning. Two dark figures nodded, bent, curtsied to each other, retreated and bowed again, lifted long arms and spread great hands against the white shadow of the screen; then with a single round movement, the sheets were folded back, disclosing two speechless men in white, standing, and another speechless man in white, lying on the bare springs of a white iron bed. The man on the springs was swathed smoothly from head to foot in white, with folded bands across the face, and a large stiff bow like merry rabbit ears dangled at the crown of his head.

The two living men lifted a mattress standing hunched against the wall, spread it tenderly and exactly over the dead man. Wordless and white they vanished down the corridor, pushing the wheeled bed before them. It had been an entrancing and leisurely spectacle, but now it was over. A pallid white fog rose in their wake insinuatingly and floated before Miranda's eyes, a fog in which was concealed all terror and all weariness, all the wrung faces and twisted backs and broken feet of abused, outraged living things, all the shapes of their confused pain and their estranged hearts; the fog might part at any moment and loose the horde of human torments. She put up her hands and said, Not yet, not yet, but it was too late. The fog parted and two executioners, white clad, moved towards her pushing between them with marvelously deft and practiced hands the misshapen figure of an old man in filthy rags whose scanty beard waggled under his opened mouth as he bowed his back and braced his feet to resist and delay the fate they had prepared for him. In a high weeping voice he was trying to explain to them that the crime of which he was accused did not merit the punishment he was about to receive; and except for this whining cry there was silence as they advanced. The soiled cracked bowls of the old man's hands were held before him beseechingly as a beggar's as he said, "Before God I am not guilty," but they held his arms and drew him onward, passed and were gone.

The road to death is a long march beset with all evils, and the heart fails little by little at each new terror, the bones rebel at each step, the mind sets up its own bitter resistance and to what end? The barriers sink one by one, and no covering of the eyes shuts out the landscape of disaster, nor the sight of crimes committed there. Across the field came Dr. Hildesheim, his face a skull beneath his German helmet, carrying a naked infant writhing on the point of his bayonet, and a huge stone pot marked Poison in Gothic letters. He stopped before the well that Miranda remembered in a pasture on her father's farm, a well once dry but now bubbling with living water, and into its pure depths he threw the child and the poison, and the violated water sank back soundlessly into the earth. Miranda, screaming, ran with her arms above her head; her voice echoed and came back to her like a wolf's howl, Hildesheim is a Boshe, a spy, a Hun, kill him, kill him before he kills you. . . . She woke howling, she heard the foul words accusing Dr. Hildesheim tumbling from her mouth; opened her eyes and knew she was in a bed in a small white room, with Dr. Hildesheim sitting beside her, two firm fingers on her pulse. His hair was brushed sleekly and his buttonhole flower was fresh. Stars gleamed through the window, and Dr. Hildesheim seemed to be gazing at them with no particular expression, his stethoscope dangling around his neck. Miss Tanner stood at the foot of the bed writing something on a chart.

"Hello," said Dr. Hildesheim, "at least you take it out in shouting. You don't try to get out of bed and go running around." Miranda held her eyes open with a terrible effort, saw his rather heavy, patient face clearly even as her mind tottered and slithered again, broke from its foundation and spun like a cast wheel in a ditch. "I didn't mean it, I never believed it, Dr. Hildesheim, you musn't remember it—" and was gone again, not being able to wait for an answer.

The wrong she had done followed her and haunted her dream: this wrong took vague shapes of horror she could not recognize or name, though her heart cringed at sight of them. Her mind, split in two, acknowledged and denied what she saw in the one instant, for across an abyss of complaining darkness her reasoning coherent self watched the strange frenzy of the other coldly, reluctant to admit the truth of its visions, its tenacious remorses and despairs.

"I know those are your hands," she told Miss Tanner, "I know it, but to me they are white tarantulas, don't touch me."

"Shut your eyes," said Miss Tanner.

"Oh, no," said Miranda, "for then I see worse things," but her eyes closed in spite of her will, and the midnight of her internal torment closed about her.

Oblivion, thought Miranda, her mind feeling among her memories of words she had been taught to describe the unseen, the unknowable, is a whirlpool of gray water turning upon itself for all eternity . . . eternity is perhaps more than the distance to the farthest star. She lay on a narrow ledge over a pit that she knew to be bottomless, though she could not comprehend it; the ledge was her childhood dream of danger, and she strained back against a reassuring wall of granite at her shoulders, staring into the pit, thinking, There it is, there it is at last, it is very simple; and soft carefully shaped words like oblivion and eternity are curtains hung before nothing at all. I shall not know when it happens, I shall not feel or remember, why can't I consent now, I am lost, there is no hope for me. Look, she told herself, there it is, that is death and there is nothing to fear. But she could not consent, still shrinking stiffly against the granite wall that was her childhood dream of safety, breathing slowly for fear of squandering breath, saying desperately, Look, don't be afraid, it is nothing, it is only eternity.

Granite walls, whirlpools, stars are things. None of them is death, nor the image of it. Death is death, said Miranda, and for the dead it has no attributes. Silenced she sank easily through deeps under deeps of darkness until she lay like a stone at the farthest bottom of life, knowing herself to be blind, deaf, speechless, no longer aware of the members of her own body, entirely withdrawn from all human concerns, yet alive with a peculiar lucidity and coherence; all notions of the mind, the reasonable inquiries of doubt, all ties of blood and the desires of the heart, dissolved and fell away from her, and there remained of her only a minute fiercely burning particle of being that knew itself alone, that relied upon nothing beyond itself for its strength; not susceptible to any appeal or inducement, being itself composed entirely of one single motive, the stubborn will to live. This fiery motionless particle set itself unaided to resist destruction, to survive and to be in its own madness of being, motiveless and planless beyond that one essential end. Trust me, the hard unwinking angry point of light said. Trust me. I stay.

At once it grew, flattened, thinned to a fine radiance, spread like a great fan and curved out into a rainbow through which Miranda, enchanted, altogether believing, looked upon a deep clear landscape of sea and sand, of soft meadow and sky, freshly washed and glistening with transparencies of blue. Why, of course, of course, said Miranda, without surprise but with serene rapture as if some promise made to her had been kept long after she had ceased to hope for it. She rose from her narrow ledge and ran lightly through the tall portals of the great bow that arched in its splendor over the burning blue of the sea and the cool green of the meadow on either hand.

The small waves rolled in and over unhurriedly, lapped upon the sand in silence and retreated; the grasses flurried before a breeze that made no sound. Moving towards her leisurely as clouds through the shimmering air came a great company of human beings, and Miranda saw in an amazement of joy that they were all the living she had known. Their faces were transfigured, each in its own beauty, beyond what she remembered of them, their eyes were clear and untroubled as good weather, and they cast no shadows. They were pure identities and she knew them every one without calling their names or remembering what relation she bore to them. They surrounded her smoothly on silent feet, then turned their entranced faces again towards the sea, and she moved among them easily as a wave among waves. The drifting circle widened, separated, and each figure was alone but not solitary; Miranda, alone too, questioning nothing, desiring nothing, in the quietude of her ecstasy, stayed where she was, eyes fixed on the over-whelming deep sky where it was always morning.

Lying at ease, arms under her head, in the prodigal warmth which flowed evenly from sea and sky and meadow, within touch but not touching the serenely smiling familiar beings about her, Miranda felt without warning a vague tremor of apprehension, some small flick of distrust in her joy; a thin frost touched the edges of this confident tranquillity; something, somebody, was missing, she had lost something, she had left something

valuable in another country, oh, what could it be? There
are no trees, no trees here, she said in fright, I have left
something unfinished. A thought struggled at the back
of her mind, came clearly as a voice in her ear. Where
are the dead? We have forgotten the dead, oh, the dead,
where are they? At once as if a curtain had fallen, the
bright landscape faded, she was alone in a strange stony
place of bitter cold, picking her way along a steep path
of slippery snow, calling out, Oh, I must go back! But
in what direction? Pain returned, a terrible compelling
pain running through her veins like heavy fire, the stench
of corruption filled her nostrils, the sweetish sickening
smell of rotting flesh and pus; she opened her eyes and
saw pale light through a coarse white cloth over her face,
knew that the smell of death was in her own body, and
struggled to lift her hand. The cloth was drawn away;
she saw Miss Tanner filling a hypodermic needle in her
methodical expert way, and heard Dr. Hildesheim saying, "I think that will do the trick. Try another." Miss
Tanner plucked firmly at Miranda's arm near the shoulder, and the unbelievable current of agony ran burning
through her veins again. She struggled to cry out, saying,
Let me go, let me go but heard only incoherent sounds
of animal suffering. She saw doctor and nurse glance at
each other with the glance of initiates at a mystery, nod-
ding in silence, their eyes alive with knowledgeable
pride. They looked briefly at their handiwork and hurried away.

Bells screamed all off key, wrangling together as they
collided in mid air, horns and whistles mingled shrilly
with cries of human distress; sulphur colored light ex-
ploded through the black window pane and flashed away
in darkness. Miranda waking from a dreamless sleep

asked without expecting an answer, "What is happening?" for there was a bustle of voices and footsteps in the corridor, and a sharpness in the air; the far clamor went on, a furious exasperated shrieking like a mob in revolt.

The light came on, and Miss Tanner said in a furry voice, "Hear that? They're celebrating. It's the Armistice. The war is over, my dear." Her hands trembled. She rattled a spoon in a cup, stopped to listen, held the cup out to Miranda. From the ward for old bedridden women down the hall floated a ragged chorus of cracked voices singing, "My country, 'tis of thee . . ."

Sweet land . . . oh, terrible land of this bitter world where the sound of rejoicing was a clamor of pain where ragged tuneless old women, sitting up waiting for their evening bowl of cocoa, were singing, "Sweet land of Liberty—"

"Oh, say, can you see?" their hopeless voices were asking next, the hammer strokes of metal tongues drowning them out. "The war is over," said Miss Tanner, her underlip held firmly, her eyes blurred. Miranda said, "Please open the window, please, I smell death in here." Now if real daylight such as I remember having seen in this world would only come again, but it is always twilight or just before morning, a promise of day that is never kept. What has become of the sun? That was the longest and loneliest night and yet it will not end and let the day come. Shall I ever see light again?

Sitting in a long chair, near a window, it was in itself a melancholy wonder to see the colorless sunlight slanting on the snow, under a sky drained of its blue. "Can this be my face?" Miranda asked her mirror. "Are these my own hands?" she asked Miss Tanner, holding them up to show the yellow tint like melted wax glimmering between the closed fingers. The body is a curious monster, no place to live in, how could anyone feel at home there? Is it possible I can ever accustom myself to this place? she asked herself. The human faces around her seemed dulled and tired, with no radiance; the once white walls of her room were now a soiled gray. Breathing slowly, falling asleep and waking again, feeling the splash of water on her flesh, taking food, talking in bare phrases with Dr. Hildesheim and Miss Tanner, Miranda looked about her with the covertly hostile eyes of an alien who does not like the country in which he finds himself, does not understand the language nor wish to learn it, does not mean to live there and yet is helpless, unable to leave it at his will.

"It is morning," Miss Tanner would say, with a sigh, for she had grown old and weary once for all in the past month, "morning again, my dear," showing Miranda the same monotonous landscape of dulled evergreens and leaden snow. She would rustle about in her starched skirts, her face bravely powdered, her spirit unbreakable as good steel, saying, "Look, my dear, what a heavenly morning, like a crystal," for she had an affection for the salvaged creature before her, the silent ungrateful human being whom she, Cornelia Tanner, a nurse who knew her business, had snatched back from death with her own hands. "Nursing is nine-tenths, just the same," Miss Tanner would tell the other nurses; "keep that in mind." Even the sunshine was Miss Tanner's own prescription for the further recovery of Miranda, this patient the doctors had given up for lost, and who yet sat here, visible proof of Miss Tanner's theory. She said, "Look at the sunshine, now," as she might be saying, "I ordered this for you, my dear, do sit up and take it."

"It's beautiful," Miranda would answer, even turning her head to look, thanking Miss Tanner for her goodness, most of all her goodness about the weather, "beautiful, I always loved it." And I might love it again if I saw it, she thought, but truth was, she could not see it. There was no light, there might never be light again, compared as it must always be with the light she had seen beside the blue sea that lay so tranquilly along the shore of her paradise. That was a child's dream of the heavenly meadow, the vision of repose that comes to a tired body in sleep, she thought, but I have seen it when I did not know it was a dream. Closing her eyes she would rest for a moment remembering that bliss which had repaid all the pain of the journey to reach it; opening them again she saw with a new anguish the dull world to which she was condemned, where the light seemed filmed over with cobwebs, all the bright surfaces corroded, the sharp planes melted and formless, all objects and beings meaningless, ah, dead and withered things that believed themselves alive!

At night, after the long effort of lying in her chair, in her extremity of grief for what she had so briefly won, she folded her painful body together and wept silently, shamelessly, in pity for herself and her lost rapture. There was no escape. Dr. Hildesheim, Miss Tanner, the nurses in the diet kitchen, the chemist, the surgeon, the precise machine of the hospital, the whole humane conviction and custom of society, conspired to pull her inseparable rack of bones and wasted flesh to its feet, to put in order her disordered mind, and to set her once more safely in the road that would lead her again to death.

Chuck Rouncivale and Mary Townsend came to see her, bringing her a bundle of letters they had guarded for her. They brought a basket of delicate small hothouse flowers, lilies of the valley with sweet peas and feathery fern, and above these blooms their faces were merry and haggard.

Mary said, "You *have* had a tussle, haven't you?" and Chuck said, "Well, you made it back, didn't you?" Then after an uneasy pause, they told her that everybody was waiting to see her again at her desk. "They've put me back on sports already, Miranda," said Chuck. For ten minutes Miranda smiled and told them how gay and what a pleasant surprise it was to find herself alive. For it will not do to betray the conspiracy and tamper with the courage of the living; there is nothing better than to be alive, everyone has agreed on that; it is past argument, and who attempts to deny it is justly outlawed. "I'll be back in no time at all," she said; "this is almost over."

Her letters lay in a heap in her lap and beside her chair. Now and then she turned one over to read the inscription, recognized this handwriting or that, examined the blotted stamps and the postmarks, and let them drop again. For two or three days they lay upon the table beside her, and she continued to shrink from them. "They will all be telling me again how good it is to be alive, they will say again they love me, they are glad I am living too, and what can I answer to that?" and her hardened, indifferent heart shuddered in despair at itself, because before it had been tender and capable of love.

Dr. Hildesheim said, "What, all these letters not opened yet?" and Miss Tanner said, "Read your letters,

my dear, I'll open them for you." Standing beside the
bed, she slit them cleanly with a paper knife. Miranda,
cornered, picked and chose until she found a thin one
in an unfamiliar handwriting. "Oh, no, now," said Miss
Tanner, "take them as they come. Here, I'll hand them
to you." She sat down, prepared to be helpful to the
end.

What a victory, what triumph, what happiness to be
alive, sang the letters in a chorus. The names were signed
with flourishes like the circles in air of bugle notes, and
they were the names of those she had loved best; some
of those she had known well and pleasantly; and a few
who meant nothing to her, then or now. The thin letter
in the unfamiliar handwriting was from a strange man
at the camp where Adam had been, telling her that Adam
had died of influenza in the camp hospital. Adam had
asked him, in case anything happened, to be sure to let
her know.

If anything happened. To be sure to let her know. If
anything happened. "Your friend, Adam Barclay,"
wrote the strange man. It had happened—she looked at
the date—more than a month ago.

"I've been here a long time, haven't I?" she asked Miss
Tanner, who was folding letters and putting them back
in their proper envelopes.

"Oh, quite a while," said Miss Tanner, "but you'll
be ready to go soon now. But you must be careful of
yourself and not overdo, and you should come back now
and then and let us look at you, because sometimes the
aftereffects are very—"

Miranda, sitting up before the mirror, wrote carefully:
"One lipstick, medium, one ounce flask Bois d'Hiver

perfume, one pair of gray suède gauntlets without straps, two pairs gray sheer stockings without clocks—"

Towney, reading after her, said, "Everything without something so that it will be almost impossible to get?"

"Try it, though," said Miranda, "they're nicer without. One walking stick of silvery wood with a silver knob."

"That's going to be expensive," warned Towney. "Walking is hardly worth it."

"You're right," said Miranda, and wrote in the margin, "a nice one to match my other things. Ask Chuck to look for this, Mary. Good looking and not too heavy." Lazarus, come forth. Not unless you bring me my top hat and stick. Stay where you are then, you snob. Not at all. I'm coming forth. "A jar of cold cream," wrote Miranda, "a box of apricot powder— and, Mary, I don't need eye shadow, do I?" She glanced at her face in the mirror and away again. "Still, no one need pity this corpse if we look properly to the art of the thing."

Mary Townsend said, "You won't recognize yourself in a week."

"Do you suppose, Mary," asked Miranda, "I could have my old room back again?"

"That should be easy," said Mary. "We stored away all your things there with Miss Hobbe." Miranda wondered again at the time and trouble the living took to be helpful to the dead. But not quite dead now, she reasured herself, one foot in either world now; soon I shall cross back and be at home again. The light will seem real and I shall be glad when I hear that someone I know has escaped from death. I shall visit the escaped ones and help them dress and tell them how lucky they are, and how lucky I am still to have them. Mary will be back soon with my gloves and my walking stick, I must go now, I must begin saying good-by to Miss Tanner and Dr. Hildesheim. Adam, she said, now you need not die again, but still I wish you were here; I wish you had come back, what do you think I came back for, Adam, to be deceived like this?

At once he was there beside her, invisible but urgently present, a ghost but more alive than she was, the last intolerable cheat of her heart; for knowing it was false she still clung to the lie, the unpardonable lie of her bitter desire. She said, "I love you," and stood up trembling, trying by the mere act of her will to bring him to sight before her. If I could call you up from the grave I would, she said, if I could see your ghost I would say, I believe . . . "I believe," she said aloud. "Oh, let me see you once more." The room was silent, empty, the shade was gone from it, struck away by the sudden violence of her rising and speaking aloud. She came to herself as if out of sleep. Oh, no, that is not the way, I must never do that, she warned herself. Miss Tanner said, "Your taxicab is waiting, my dear," and there was Mary. Ready to go.

No more war, no more plague, only the dazed silence that follows the ceasing of the heavy guns; noiseless houses with the shades drawn, empty streets, the dead cold light of tomorrow. Now there would be time for everything.